MAGICKS
& MYSTICISM

Magicks & Mysticism is a work of fiction. References to real people, events, establishments, organizations, or locales are intended only to provide the sense of authenticity and are use fictitiously. All other characters, all incidents, dialogue are drawn from the author's imagination and are not to be seen as real.

Copyright © 2022. All rights reserved.

Also available in hardcover and eBook.

Published by Dark Titan Publishing. A division of Dark Titan Entertainment.

Dark Titan Universe is a branch of Dark Titan Entertainment.

Hardcover ISBN: 979-8-9866393-4-5
Paperback ISBN: 979-8-9866393-2-1
eBook ISBN: 979-8-9866393-3-8

darktitanentertainment.com

WORKS BY TY'RON W. C. ROBINSON II

BOOKS/SHORT STORIES

DARK TITAN UNIVERSE SAGA

MAIN SERIES
Dark Titan Knights
The Resistance Protocol
Tales of the Scattered
Tales of the Numinous
Day of Octagon
Crossbreed
Heaven's Called
The Oranos Imperative
Underworld

SPIN-OFFS
In A Glass of Dawn: The Casebook of Travis Vail
Maveth: Bloodsport
The Curse of The Mutant-Thing
Trail of Vengeance
War of The Thunder Gods

ONE-SHOTS
Maveth, The Death-Bringer Mystery of The Mutant-Thing Shade & Switchblade
Retribution of Cain
The Mythologists
Ambush Bot
Kang-Zhu
Cheeseburger Man
Tessa Balthazar
Elite 5

COLLECTIONS
Dark Titan Omnibus: Volume 1
Dark Titan Omnibus: Volume 2
Dark Titan One-Shot Collection
Dark Titan One-Shot Collection II

THE HAUNTED CITY SAGA
The Legendary Warslinger: The Haunted City I
Battle of Astolat: A Haunted City Prequel (KOBO Exclusive)
Redemption of the Lost: The Haunted City II
Helper's Hand: A Haunted City One-Shot

SYMBOLUM VENATORES
Symbolum Venatores: The Gabriel Kane Collection
Hod: A Symbolum Venatores Book
Symbolum Venatores: War of The Two Kingdoms
Symbolum Venatores: Elrad's Chronicles
Symbolum Venatores Collection

EVERWAR UNIVERSE
EverWar Universe: Knights & Lords
Avior vs. Dekar

PRODIGIOUS WORLDS
Mark Porter of Argoron
Raiders of Vanok
Praxus of Lithonia

FRIGHTENED! SERIES
Frightened!: The Beginning

INSTINCTS SERIES
Lost in Shadows: Remastered
Instincts Point Hope

THE HORDE TRILOGY
The Horde
The Dreaded Ones

DARK TITAN'S THE DEAD DAYS
Accounts of The Dead Days

OTHER BOOKS
The Book of The Elect
The Extended Age Omnibus
The Eleventh Hour: A Chevah Mythos Story
The Supreme Pursuer: Darkness of the Hunt
Massacre in the Dusk
Venture into Horror: Tales of the Supernatural
The Universe of Realms Omnibus: Book 1
The Universe of Realms Omnibus: Book 2

THE DARK TITAN AUDIO EXPERIENCE PODCAST
Season 1: Introductions
Season 2: In a Glass of Dawn
Season 2.5: Accounts of The Dead Days
Season 3: Battle For Astolat
Season 4: Hallow Sword: Cursed

DARK TITAN UNIVERSE SAGA
MAGICKS & MYSTICISM

TY'RON W. C. ROBINSON II

CONTENTS

CREED: HELL RISEN
1

DEATH CHASER: DEADLY PROTECTOR
11

TRAVIS VAIL, SPIRIT-SEEKER: THE PAST AND THE FUTURE
28

THE DEVILHUNTER: COVEN OF DREAD
44

THE MAN CALLED FABLE: MAGIC AND SEEK
59

DOCTOR FORTUNE: SPIRITUAL GODFARE
65

DOCTOR DARK: DIMENSIONS AND SEASONS
89

HEAVEN HAS CALLED: MAGICKS & MYSTICISM
114

CREED: HELL RISEN

I

BURNING SENSATION

One night across the city of Hartford, Connecticut in the span of only a few hours, calls were rung in to the authorities over a mass murder. The murders had seemed to be committed all at one time across the entire city. Even into the suburb areas. With the police unable to track down a concrete source to continue their investigation, hovering over the city throughout the bleak clouds was Creed, The Unholy Knight. Gleaming down toward the city, Creed moved with speed and a supernatural form of stealth. His appearance unseen by the eyes of the living due to the illusion conjured by his flowing midnight-blue cape.

"These bodies." Creed examined. "They're charred. Poor souls."

The victims were all burnt. Their skin bubbling continually as the sound of cracks sparked. Even in the presence of the officers and coroners. The heat coming from their bodies was too hot for the coroners to continue their work further. Choosing to leave the bodies in their discovered state, Creed searched them all. Seeing every body was burnt in similar fashion. Knowing it all took place at one time, Creed knew there wasn't a natural solution to the cause. Hearing the willowing sound from behind him, Creed rose up from his knee, seeing Ananchel standing beside him looking down over the bodies. Beaming of light.

"You've found them." She said.

"I have. These weren't natural deaths. Something reeks of this cause."

"I know who's responsible. But, you're not familiar with the murderer."

"Speak the name."

"You smell the stench in the air?"

"I do. Smells of brimstone. Only hellfire could've done such a thing."

"Sinfire also has its bidding." Ananchel mentioned. "However, you are correct. Hellfire is the cause of their deaths. The officers won't be able to answer the families of the victims with sound information."

"They will do what they can." Creed said. "Meanwhile, you said you know who's responsible. Tell me who."

"A demon. Calls itself *Brimstone*."

"Leaving its mark for us to find. Not a smart demon."

"Don't think of him lightly. Brimstone has been around through the ages. He's responsible for great fires in the ancient past. Myself and the Cherubim did our best to cool his wrath. Fortunately, we did, and he was driven into hiding."

"And now he's risen again to cause more hell." Creed spoke. "By what means has caused him to be risen?"

"I do not know. Perhaps, he's risen due to the growing power of the Cryptic Zone."

"You believe Adrambadon has a hand in this?"

"I'm not saying such. Only implying the Zone is surging with power. All of the air across the earth is mucked in mysticism. Most of us are not sure why nor do we know the source's location."

Creed took another look at the bodies and he watched as the officers continued their work to the best of their ability. The coroners even went to the point of dousing water over the bodies to cool them. Yet, the water only increased their burnt nature with sparks emitting from the cracked skin.

"What must be done?" Creed asked.

"Brimstone moves with speed. Speed beyond most of ours. Yet, you may be able to catch up to him."

"Do you have a precise location of his whereabouts?"

"I do not. I know he likes a challenge. Given by any means, he'll accept a challenge if it deems itself powerful enough to test him."

"His figure? What does this Brimstone appear to be?"

"Unlike Satanic, he's not a dog-like being. More so one of them."

"He's in the image like the sons of Adam?"

"Yes. Appearing like one of them is what gives him an edge."

"And I'm assuming he's burning in nature?"

"Like a flowing volcano after an explosion."

Creed took a nod and flew into the air, searching Hartford. Through his eyes, he spotted an open field. The moment was set in motion.

"I'll call him out. See what he's made of."

"And where will you do this?" Ananchel wondered.

"There's an open field over in the distance. Far from humans. There, I shall call out this Brimstone and end his little run."

"Calling him out is a challenge he'll accept."

"You know of this?" Creed wondered. "You're saying such an act is simple for him?"

"He loves challenges. Once you call him out, he'll appear. He can't resist."

II

THE WARNING OF THE UNDERWORLD

Creed flown into the open field. Nothing but trees surrounding him. Stretching out his arms, Creed began to recite a ritual in the language of the Cryptic Zone. The ground trembled as it cracked open, unveiling the glooming glow of the Cryptic Zone. Through such power, Creed was able to expand his power, absorbing the energy flowing from the Cryptic Zone into his being. Closing his hands together, the cracks sealed and the trembles ceased.

"Brimstone! I summon you to this place! Leave humanity be and face me!"

Through the quietness of the wind circling the field, the ground quaked once more, however not through Creed's own power. Certain of this, Creed's gaze turned every corner as through the ground erupted a geyser of flames. Standing back as his cape shielded him from the fires, within them stepped out Brimstone himself. Creed paused as his cape moved from his eyes, Brimstone's appearance was just as Ananchel told him.

"This is the famed Unholy Knight." Brimstone growled.

"I am he you have spoke. See you've come to my calling."

"Indeed I have. I can only believe Ananchel gave you such an idea to begin with. Although, it is a pity she couldn't do the work herself. Nor any of the angels above."

"Your business is with me. Not with the angels."

"I am aware. Yet, you have to be wondering why I've come at such a strange time."

"You killed those innocents. Burned their bodies to cinders."

"Only to gain someone's attention. Didn't matter whose it was, only that my work received its reward."

"A reward of what nature?" Creed questioned. "A treasure?"

"I have no need of treasures. I sought out another in the spiritual warfare and you answered the call."

"You sought out a battle. To test your own skills against another."

"Yes. And what better skills to be tested than the Cryptic powers against the fires of Hell itself!"

Creed's claws formed over his fingers as his cape whipped across the air, Bellowing a powerful gust against Brimstone as the fires covering his body wisped away, slowly reappearing in mass as the embers emerged. Brimstone waved his hand while shaking his head. A grin of sinister faces grew on his face. Creed's eyes remained focus.

"You haven't truly questioned the reason for all of this." Brimstone said. "Your battle against Medieval proved to all of us that you have such skills yet to be fully revealed."

"How do you know about Medieval?"

"Because we know everyone and their reasons in such fields. Medieval deals with warfare while I tend to the flames. It's only nature in action."

"I've heard enough. I'm ending your actions above this ground."

"Do your best. However, why don't we take it below."

"Below?" Creed said.

Brimstone raised his arms, causing the ground to tremble. The trembles increased as Creed leaped up into the air to maintain his balance. Gazing down, he saw the ground had opened and through his eyes, he was looking into Hell itself. Brimstone chuckled at the sight, whipping fire into his hands.

"Let us see if the cryptic power can match the fires of Hell!"

Moving like lightning, Brimstone struck Creed in the face with the fire blast and dragged the Unholy Knight down into the pit. Once they were several feet deep, the ground above them had sealed. Now, Creed crashed onto the ground, surrounded by flames. The flames were the color of his cape and sparked like the gold of his eyes. Creed stood up and took a moment to see his surroundings as Brimstone was nowhere to be found.

"Ah." Creed said. "So this is Hell."

III

HELLFIRE

Creed hovered over the fires of Hell, hearing the fainted cries of the souls within the burning flames. Gazing down over them, he could recognize their human nature as they shouted to him to warn their families. Creed hung his head hearing their cries for the living. However, Creed knew his words wouldn't matter to the living and he continued searching for Brimstone.

"Where is he?" Creed questioned within.

A gusher of flames emitted from the fire in front of Creed, hitting him from below as he tumbled through the air, regaining his balance. Taking a look around the flames and the molten rock surrounding him, Brimstone rushed toward him like a lightning bolt of fire, striking him in the chest with a deepening punch. Creed fell and crashed onto the ground, surrounded by the sapphire-glowing flames as Brimstone stepped down in front of him.

"Welcome to my domain!" Brimstone cocked.

"It appears you are afraid of what's above. Proclaiming this prison as your domain."

"Me and the fires are one. Otherwise, I would not exist."

"And you sought to attack those of the earth only for the pursuit of a challenge."

"A challenge which you accepted. Now, shall we continue this bout before you give in to your own concerns."

"I will defeat you, demon and afterwards, I will cleanse the disturbance you have brought upon those families."

"Heh. Good luck with that."

Brimstone and Creed clashed with blows to the jaws and chest. Jumping back a few feet, Brimstone rushed against Creed with his heel, striking Creed in the face and latching his hands to Creed's ankles, tripping him onto reground as his face came close to the burning fires. With a quick grunt, Creed kicked himself up and conjured a sword from his hands, impressing Brimstone.

"You think you're the only one who can wield such power?!"

Brimstone repeated Creed's own actions, forming a molten sword from his hands. Creed held his steady as Brimstone leaped into the air, crashing down against Creed's sword. The two struggled against one another with their strength. Creed's golden eyes flickered as Brimstone's face morphed between human and demon forms. Droplets of fire fell from Brimstone's head onto Creed's face, burning him for a few seconds. Creed shoved Brimstone from him, twirling the blade as he cut Brimstone's chest with the tip of the sword. A chuckle came out of Brimstone's mouth before he slashed Creed's abdomen with his own sword, burning him in the process.

"I'm not even tired, Cryptic One!"

"Neither am I."

Creed's cape bellowed around him before spanning out like wings of a great dragon, picking up the fires from around them and tossing them against Brimstone. The fiery demon used his sword to swipe down the incoming fireballs as Creed took the chance and speared Brimstone against the molten walls with his sword.

"Argh!" Brimstone grunted. "You think this will defeat me?!"

"No." Creed answered. "But it gives me the chance to keep you down here. At least for a while."

Creed raised his right hand, from his sharp fingertips emerged a golden hue of energy. Taking the focus of the energy, Creed directed it from his hand toward Brimstone. The golden energy warped into a liquid form, seemly unharmed by the flames of Hell. Brimstone pulled the sword from his shoulder as the energy surrounded him. Wrapping itself around him against eh wall like a snake to its prey. Feeling the tightness of the energy, Brimstone yelled with a deepen scream. Not one of pain, but of anger.

"What is this?!" Brimstone screamed. "What have you done?!"

"I've used a portion of my Cryptic powers to trap you here. In Hell."

"You cannot trap me! I was formed from this realm!"

"I know and the power of the Cryptic Zone will make sure you remain here until the end of days."

"No. No! I will not be trapped by some disgruntled figure! A human made into a Crypticzoid!"

Creed turned away, looking up toward what appeared to be a sparking light. Creed focused on the light through Brimstone's continued yelling and flew into the air toward the light. Inching closer, Creed discovered the light was a pathway for him to return to the earth and he went through the light, quickly finding himself above the ground and in the skies overlooking the field where he fell into the pit. Seeing the field, Creed noticed there was no hole where he fell.

"I'm back."

Hearing wings behind him, Creed quickly turned to see Ananchel moving with a haste in her flight. Her face slightly bruised with her wings bleeding from beneath and claw makes against her chest armor. Her eyes only told of a horror Creed had never seen. Ananchel attempted to keep her balance in the air, yet she fell to the ground. Creed flew down and caught her before she crashed.

"What happened?" Creed asked. "What's going on?"

"Something's wrong… the powers… they've been… altered."

"Powers? What powers?"

"The mystical energy that surrounds the universe. Something has altered them and now, they've been awoken."

"Who's been awoken?"

"The Dark Gods. I tried to help the sorcerer, but their powers were too great."

"Sorcerer?"

"Go now, Creed and help him."

"Help who?"

"*The Supreme Enchanter. Doctor Fortune.*"

DEATH CHASER DEADLY PROTECTOR

I

SEEK FOR THE TRUTH

Ongoing civilians have declared a widespread of nightmares occurring in their sleep. Nightmares which are appearing to grow rapidly each night. The reports state each night, the nightmares become more intense to the point of the sleeper awakening to the visual effects of the dream. With psychiatrists and doctors all ruling out supernatural occurrences to the victims affected, suggesting their nightmares are only a concern due to their own mental state. However, a few civilians have awoken late in the night and encountered a shadow figure lurking in their home the day before their nightmare took place.

Moving through the dimensions was the Death Chaser. After dealing with the three demons sent to him by Dieheart and uncovering more information which concerns Demonticronto's coming resurgence, the Chaser continued his work in the arts of spiritual warfare. Remembering the words spoken during his recent alignment with Heaven's Called against Vernon Lance and the Mythologists, the Chaser knew he had to do more to ensure the protection of the innocent. Feeling the energy growing from the nightmares, the Chaser summoned himself into the small town and searched it throughout. From every home, store, and local place where the people dwelt.

"The touch." The Chaser said to himself. "It is not of Nightmare. Nor of the Bogeyman. Ah. This is something else. Something… different."

Taking into account the information he gained, the Chaser rode out of the small town, heading to another location where he was being summoned. Summoned in fact by Robin Knight and Widow.

II

A UNIFIED EVIL

Robin Knight and Widow sat inside a small cabin deep within the woodlands of the Northern United States. While they sat and talked about the recent events and their meeting with Madame LoCasta, they heard the roaring sound of flames outside the door. Robin Knight arose from his chair and slowly approached the door. Nearly within two feet from the door, it opened itself as the Chaser stood present. Robin Knight exhaled with relief as the Chaser entered the cabin.

"I know you were expecting me."

"Not this soon." Robin said. "However, you're here now."

"As I always appear. There's something happening to the people. Nightmares. Unusual nightmares. The more progress as each day passes."

"Do you think it's a nightmare demon?" Widow asked.

"It isn't. I dealt with Nightmare some time ago. It's something else."

"Wait." John said. "You mean there's an entity called Nightmare?"

"No need to concern yourself with him. He's been dealt with."

Robin went ahead and sat down at the table. The Chaser leaned against the wall, his face reverting from his skull form to his human appearance. Robin stared and Widow was in awe. They saw the Chaser in his full human form and he smirked.

"What?"

"It's just we've never seen you like this."

"Because I'm human. My name's Danny Logan."

"So, you're human after all." Widow said. "Wow."

John stepped closer toward Danny. Looking at this attire, seeing the scorches still from the flames. Danny grinned and chuckled under his breath seeing the amazement coming from John and Widow.

"You're human." John said. "Just like us."

"I am."

"But, how do you turn into the Death Chaser? I've read that Chaser were once human. Never expected one to be able to revert back and forth."

"Throughout the ages, there have been many Death Chasers. I am certain I will not be the last one. Yet, for the times we're in, I am the Death Chaser of this age. What happened to me was a confrontation. I wanted to make the world better by any means of my skills. One night, I was visited by a spirit who promised me such a task. I accepted and three days later, I began to burn from within. The fires became to intense and I transformed into the Death Chaser. Once the transformation was complete, I knew my mission in this life and I've been living it ever since."

"And you've been going across the world? Saving people?" Widow wondered.

"I have. Some incidents are human-based. Others are more of a supernatural occurrence. The Death Chaser does what he must in those situations. Whatever the cost."

"And you're the only one?" John asked.

"There are many. Only location and purpose separate one from the other."

While speaking, a rushing wind bolted the door open, Danny

quickly reverted into his Death Chaser form as a black mist entered, circling around Widow. John was unsure as to what the mist could be. The Chaser, sensing the malevolent energy, raised his hands as they were covered in sin fire and snatched the mist from around Widow.

"I know of this!" The Chaser said, struggling with the mist.

John stood up from his seat, prepared for a fight as two more forces entered through the door. One in the form of a lycan yet appeared more of a hound than wolf. The other showed itself as an upright figure, gleaming in shiny emerald. John stepped back, seeing the two. The Chaser's eyes glinted toward them and from there he knew who they were.

"Dream Seeker." The Chaser said toward the emerald wearer.

"You remember me."

"And you bring pawns to do your work."

The mist pulled from the grasp of the Chaser and retreated outside to the sound of a quickening howl. Upon the silence which followed, footsteps sounded as they approached the door. Standing beside Dream Seeker was a man of lean stature, his skin covered in diverse tattoos of animals, torture techniques, and demons. His eyes were solid black and he grinned with a sinister expression.

"Did my little trick soothe you?"

"I know what you are." The Chaser said. "You're a reanimator."

"What's a reanimator?" John questioned.

"One who can conjure images into reality. Although, looking at his physique, he can bring forth his markings into reality."

"Look, we all have our reasons for being here. Right now, I have some work to do. Chaser, you're trespassing in my affairs with your disciples."

"I will not allow you to escape, Seeker of Dreams."

The Chaser roared as flames emerged from his hands and

mouth. Seeking to strike down the Dream Seeker, only for the entity to vanish through a puff of emerald mist. As the mist fell to the ground, John and Widow looked out and even saw the two others were gone. The Chaser came to his senses, seeing the three adversaries had disappeared. Letting out a roar of anger, the Chaser vowed to find the Dream Seeker and to eliminate him alongside his two followers whom he deemed as Bloodhound and the Ink Man.

III
PROPHECY OF THE TIMES

The Chaser came up with a plan. A plan to stop the Dream Seeker, Bloodhound, and Ink Man. Now, he knew he couldn't take them all by himself, although such action would be a casual affair for a Death Chaser. Instead, he commanded for John and Widow to track down Ink Man as he would search for Bloodhound, whom would immediately lead him to Dream Seeker.

Walking through the wilderness not far from the cabin, John and Widow quickly became the hunted by one of Ink Man's living tattoos. Making a run for it as the shadow of a wolf began to chase them through the darkness of the forest. Dodging through the shadowed trees as the rustling breath of the wolf echoed behind them. They came to a stopping point and hid behind two trees. Both covered with leaves even near to the ground. The wolf rushed into place and paused. Raising its shadowed nose to the air. The air had no scent to John or Widow. The wolf howled before continuing further into the forest. Widow sighed.
"We need to find the Chaser." John said. "Quickly."

In another part of the forest, the Death Chaser walked with a shroud of calmness. Taking his steps slowly, he could hear the fainting wisp around him from Bloodhound. The gurgling breaths came from the bushes in front of him as his right hand glowed with sinfire. The Chaser stood still as the fire burned, droplets fell to the dirt, searing the downed leaves around him into a circle of flame. Just in that moment, the Bloodhound bolted from the bushes with its jaws wide open. The Chaser extended his arm in the air, blasting a ball of sinfire into the face of Bloodhound. The creature fell to the ground, twirling in the dirt as it burned. The Chaser glared down at the creature before snatching it by its throat and tossing it deeper into the woods. Far from where he stood. Watching Bloodhound vanish in mid-air, the Chaser sighed and turned around to meet with John and Widow. While making his return, he was stopped by a woman standing in the forest. His hand glowed with fire once more.

"No need to harm me, Soul of Retribution."

"A woman appears in the woods unannounced. Unseen. Am I meant to take this as a light matter?"

"No. you are correct to react in such a manner."

"Who are you?"

"I am Madame LoCasta. I spoke with two of your associates some time ago."

The Chaser sighed. Not with relief, but of anger.

"You're the fortune teller. The one who delves in the forbidden arts of Man."

"I do not practice malevolent magic. Only the ones in which help my fellow man."

"Magic is magic."

"I have only appeared before you to give you a warning. A warning regarding the near and vast future."

"A warning? Are you threatening me, witch?"

"No threat. Just want to give you some knowledge I possess of what's about to happen."

"Go ahead. Tell me your fortune."

"You will save John and the Widow from the Tattooed Man. You will face the Dream Seeker and shall defeat him. After, you will be reunited with past colleges against a great evil before you return to discover a more darker power has arrived. One involved in your past."

"Sounds to me you talk of Demonticronto."

"The devilish one is not whom I speak of. But of another. One you have yet to face."

"And how does this mysterious entity connect to my past? In what fashion or form?"

"I cannot tell you. Yet, take my words as only of knowledge. Guard them for the time ahead. They will guide you."

"I don't need your guidance. Much less from a witch."

"Again." LoCasta sighed. "I am not a witch. Only a helper to humanity in ways the modern world frown upon."

The Chaser's hands grew with more sinfire as he dropped the ball of flames to the ground, creating a portal. Before taking his step in, LoCasta informed him of John and Widow's precise location. The Chaser took her words. As much as he could muster before entering the portal. When the portal closed, LoCasta was gone from the forest.

John and Widow had found their way back to the cabin. Just before making their way inside, the leaves behind them blew into the air, startling Widow as the Ink Man made himself known, morphing from the dirt beneath the leaves. He stretched himself to the sound of popping bones.

"Did you think you escaped my sight?"

"We did our best." John said. "Anyhow, we'll take you on."

The Ink Man stretched his arm, pointing toward the ground.

His fists opened as the tattoos upon his forearms tore from him and fell to the ground. One was the shadowed wolf which chased them and the other was a shadowed bear.

"Let's see if you can handle two beasts on your own."

"Widow, go inside." John said.

"I can help."

"Let me. You keep yourself guarded. We're not sure if the Chaser stopped the other one."

The Ink Man's shadowed creatures snarled toward John as he pulled out his staff. Once Widow took one step into the cabin door, the searing sound of flames moved through the air. The Ink Man grinned as he turned around to see the Chaser standing, his hands shrouded in fire.

"You believe your sinfire can scorch my works of art?"

"Sinfire can purge all things." The Chaser whipped the flames from his hands.

The shadowed wolf lunged toward the Chaser under the Ink Man's command. The wolf went for the neck, only to be swiped into the ground and evaporated by the sudden appearance of a burning chain. A chain made from the sinfire itself. The sight of the burning chain brought fear into the Ink Man's being. Stepping back as the shadowed bear went for an attack. The Chaser raised the searing chain and slashed the shadowed bear in half, evaporating the creature into nothing but a bellowing mist of embers.

"You don't think I have more the bring forth?! My body is covered with beasts and monsters beyond the sights of men."

"I believe you." The Chaser replied.

With quick whips, the chain swiped the body of the Ink Man. Scorching his skin and the tattoos which were dormant. With each attack, the Ink Man became slower to move. Stiff to lift up his arms and sluggish to conjure more shadow beings. The Chaser continued to burn every tattoo he could see, bringing the Ink Man to his knees.

"You have been defeated." The Chaser said.

"No kidding. I can't, I can't continue to do this."

"It seems your boastfulness was burned as well. Tell me one thing. Where's the Dream Seeker?"

"It is not simple to understand."

"Try me."

The Ink Man scoffed and grunted from the burning upon his body. The scent of his scorched skin began to move through the forest, brining attention of their presence to the animals which dwelled around them.

"You must enter the mind of a dreamer in order to face him. It is how I was recruited for this cause."

"Thank you." The Chaser said before sending the Ink Man through a burning portal into an unknown region.

The portal had closed once John and Widow were making their way toward the Chaser.

"Where did you send him?"

"Somewhere in which he can reassess his path and his markings."

"Now what do we do?" John questioned. "How can we find the Dream Seeker?"

"The Inked One said to enter the mind of a dreamer to face the Seeker." The Chaser replied. "I know what he meant."

"Tell us please."

"It means you have to enter the mind of one who's asleep." Widow spoke.

John turned toward her with a curious gaze. He didn't realize she might've known what was spoken by the Ink Man. The Chaser agreed with her and began to come up with a plan to enter the realm of the dreaming. Before he could utter another world, Widow stopped him.

"I know what we must do. You know what we have to do. I

will be the dreamer."

"You can't do that to yourself." John said.

"My mind is much clearer during sleep. It is the best way to confront the Dream Seeker. Besides, he took notice of me. He might know what we're about to do."

"That makes no difference." The Chaser said. "We've wasted enough time. Let's begin."

The three returned inside the cabin and Widow laid upon the bed and fell asleep. While she slept, John questioned the Chaser as to how they would enter her mind. The chaser stood up beside the bed and conjured another flaming portal on the floor. John stood on the other end. From there, the Chaser placed his palm on the Widow's forehead before taking one step into the portal. John watched as the portals imagery changed. showing a collage of staircases and on one of them he saw Widow running.

"She's there."

"Step into the portal, John."

John took a step into the portal and the two were drawn in like a rushing wind. Now, they stood on the stop of a staircase surrounded by what seemed to be outer space as the other dozen staircases circled around them. The Chaser to a gander to the location. A place he's known of and yet never seen. John searched for Widow and saw her ahead of them in the distance. He went to make a run before Chaser grabbed his arm.

"What is it?"

"Do not be hasty in this place. He knows we're here."

The surroundings let out a haunting laugh muffled beneath the walls of the dreaming. They both knew it was the Dream Seeker making his entrance.

"Prepare yourself for battle. It is the only way we get this finished."

IV

DREAMS ARE WHAT WE MAKE THEM

The Chaser and Robin Knight moved with complete stealth as above them roamed the shadow of the Dream Seeker. He was now within the mind of Widow, searching for her true desires both good and evil. John kept his hand prepared for the battle as did the Chaser, who's eyes glinted at every turn from the Seeker. Taking every step cautiously to avoid contact from the Dream Seeker, Widow turned around as she ran through the numbering staircases. Seeing the Chaser and John in the distance, a smile formed and with that, the Dream Seeker fully manifested in her mind, landing on a staircase in between them.

"Oh no." John whispered.

"Don't play stealth with me, Chaser. I know you're here."

The Chaser arose from the shadows and faced the Seeker. John followed the Chaser's motives and rose up from hiding to stand beside him. The Dream Seeker scoffed at John's appearance with a laugh.

"You brought a mortal with you? In this place?"

"He's closer with the Widow. He has a right to be here. Unlike yourself."

"You're mistaken. I roam the Dreamscape. It is my purpose of existence. You know this. Just as it is your duty to purge the material realm of malevolent forces and sin-filled disasters, mine is to occupy the mind of the dreamers. All of them and in due time, I shall reap my reward."

The Chaser's hands sparked with fire as the chain formed within it, landing on the ground in between them. The head of the chain was detailed with a scythe. The Chaser turned to John, looking at his hands.

"Where are your weapons?"

"I didn't bring them. They're inside the cabin."

The Chaser waved his right hand over John's, thereby conjuring his weapons from the cabin. John scoffed as he held them tightly. His focus centered on the Dream Seeker as was the Chaser's.

"You truly desired to do this?" The Dream Seeker asked.

"It is the only option." John yelled.

The Dream Seeker nodded before shattering himself into emerald pieces. Scattering across the realm of the dreaming. The Chaser moved with speed, whipping flames toward the pieces and melting them in the air.

"Go for Widow!" The Chaser yelled.

"What?"

"Go! Sand with her while I handle the Seeker. Protect her from any kind of attack. Whether from the Seeker or herself!"

"What do you mean by her?"

"This place is her mind. Good and evil dwell here." The Chaser answered while burning more shattered pieces of emerald. "Now, go and protect her."

John obeyed the words of the Chaser and went to reach her while dodging the coming attacks from the Seeker's shards. Deflecting them with his own swords while the Chaser continued to burn them. He jumped from staircase to staircase while admiring the starry surroundings in which he stood. Seeing

Widow up ahead, he began to run down the pathway of concrete before being stopped by a shadow figure. Falling to the ground, John looked up as the shadow figure manifested into a void of himself.

"The hell are you?"

"I am you. A darker perception from Widow's mind. A reflection of what you hold within."

"I don't think I do."

"Widow can see things you cannot. She can sense the motives and desires in people. She hides this ability well. Others have called it discernment."

"I know what discernment is. But, I'm not you and you're not me. You're just a shadow."

John swung the sword, slashing through the shadow to no avail. The shadow grinned as John realized there was no impact. He went for another swipe and it was only a repeat of seconds prior. The shadow John stretched his arms forward, shoving John back near where he first entered. His eyes squinting from the rushing wind as he could see Widow watching him.

"Stop him!" John screamed. "Stop him!"

Widow watched as John continued to hold himself against his shadow doppelganger. Widow proceeded to take a step forward behind the shadow John, reaching for John himself to grab her hand. He saw it and pressed forward against the wind. Behind him, the Chaser continued to break down the emerald shards bolting through the air as the laughter of the Seeker echoed through the dreaming realm.

"Take my hand!" Widow yelled.

John continued to press against the wind and he forced himself to rush through his shadow form, blowing it back as he grabbed Widow's hand. Once the two came into contact, the shadow John vanished to the distraught of the Seeker as his face shrouded over them in the air. His eyes kindling with a burning emerald.

"You will proceed to see the darkness of your mind. It is the only way you can overcome your grieves."

"Not with your help."

The Seeker gathered the remaining shards out of the sight of the Chaser and formed them back into himself. Landing in front of John and Widow. The Chaser saw them in the distance and ran to reach them. John swung his sword toward the Seeker, only chipping off small fragments of emerald before quickly being grabbed by his throat and held up.

"Let him go!" Widow said as the Seeker stared at her.

"The only pitiful thing bout this is I cannot harm you. If I do, not only will you be damaged, but so will I. can't let that happen. So, woman, give in to your true desires and become my soldier in the material realm. Do the work of the dreaming. Become an apostle to the Dream Seeker."

"I cannot. No!" Widow yelled. "I will not become a servant of yours. You will leave my mind and never return."

"I will leave once you become one of mine."

"She told you to leave." The Chaser's voice echoed from behind.

The Seeker turned as the Chaser lunged toward him, holding him by his throat and face. The hands of the Chaser sparked into flames as he melted the head of the Seeker into a puddle of burning emerald. His body exploded into the air and moved chaotic through the air. The Chaser knew this would happened and raised his arms to the sky and from them came a large combustion of sinfire, consuming the emerald fragments into dust. Once the sound of the explosion whispered away, the Chaser nodded to John as he approached Widow.

"It is time for you to wake up."

Widow nodded and looked behind her, seeing a door. A door made of glowing mist and within it was nothing but light.

Brighter than the sun. She looked at the Chaser for clarity and he nodded. She took her steps toward the door and as she approached it, she paused. Taking a look back to see the Chaser and John disappearing from her sight. From there, she stepped into the door and within seconds she awoke. Laying on the bed inside the cabin with the Chaser and John standing by her side.

"Is that it?" She questioned.

"For now." The Chaser replied. "I only purged him from your mind. He still lingers in other parts of the world."

"So, he'll be back?" John questioned.

"No. He won't. as long as she's around, he cannot return."

Widow nodded with a smile.

"Thank you."

"It is my purpose. He was correct on that."

The sound of a blast of wind hit the cabin door and it opened. John immediately turned and held his sword in hand. Widow remained on the bed, moving behind John as the Chaser slowly took one step forward. After the step, a calmness touched him. He Chaser told John to lower his sword to his own confusion.

"Are you sure?" John asked.

"I am. We're not in danger."

Standing at the door was the Visitant Outlander. His eyes glowing and a nod he granted.

"Why have you come to see me, Outlander?" The Chaser questioned.

"You are needed to help an ally in the field."

"Which ally do you speak of?"

"The Supreme Enchanter, Doctor Fortune." The Outlander answered. "He needs your help."

TRAVIS VAIL, SPIRIT-SEEKER: THE PAST AND THE FUTURE

I

ROME OF THE WEST

On a cold and sunny day in St. Louis, Missouri, Travis Vail had entered the gates to the city. Vail's purpose of arriving in the city was due to a call he received from his mentor, Dr. Galen Donovan about a proposed haunting moving through a particular region of the city. Vail had once driven through St. Louis in the past, yet he never stayed nor wondered if the city had any haunting to it. Demons? Sure. But, the occasional haunting? Never lingered in the mind of the Spirit-Seeker.

Vail drove through the city, arriving at the Central Library. Walking inside as he saw Donovan and his colleague, Colton Levi sitting at a table. They saw Vail approaching and stood up to greet their friend. Sitting down after their greeting, Vail was immediately interested in the case. His expression could be seen by nearing everyone in the library. Galen smiled.

"You're eager to know more aren't you?" Colton asked.

"In a way, I am." Vail smirked. "So, what's happening in this place?"

"Hauntings of history." Galen answered. "Those affected have said to have seen glimpses into the past and the future."

"You're serious?"

"Serious as can be." Colton said. "The people we talked to said they saw glimpses of Ancient Rome."

"Fitting." Vail replied. "Seeing as how we're in the Rome of the West. Makes a connection in a way."

"That's not all." Galen said. "While some saw the past in just landmarks, others saw events. Events such as the burning of the Library of Alexandria, wars of the Crusades, even the parting of the Red Sea."

Vail nodded.

"Well then, they had the opportunity of seeing spectacles. One thing I must ask. What you're both telling me are events which connect to the past. What about those who have seen the future?"

"One man we spoke to said he saw the future. Countries we know of today no longer existed. Soldiers were automated and humanity was changed completely."

"I know the telling. But, how is this connected to the supernatural? From what I've gathered by your information, these glimpses could be the simple workings of a sage, fortune teller, or even some kind of techno-geek. It's all technology based is what I can tell."

"He has a point, Dr. Donovan." Colton said.

"He does. Well, that's all we can give you. I'm sure you want to know if there's a history on this."

"There has to be. Besides, we're in a museum. Isn't there something here that may connect all of this. Besides the artifacts."

"While you were arriving into the city, Raynard went to the Central Library to do some studying. Perhaps you'll want to meet with him there. See what he uncovers."

"As I always do." Vail stood up from the table. "Are you two staying in town or are you leaving already?"

"Do you need our help on this one?" Colton asked. "Or are

you other friends here elsewhere?"

Vail gave them a look. They knew the look and grinned.

"My 'friends' as you call them, are dealing with their own matters elsewhere. Besides, I'm sure you'll meet them eventually."

"I'm intrigued to meet this Doctor you've encountered. They call him the Supreme Enchanter, right?"

"It's a lineage title." Vail said. "Nothing more to me."

"Contact me when you've solved it." Galen replied.

"I will."

Vail left the museum and traveled to the Central Library where he found Raynard Brown, his trusty historian going through the books. Connecting the dots to the case. He raised up his head to see Vail standing in front of him, grinning.

"You could've said something."

"I thought about that. But, I wouldn't disturb a man such as you in your work. Could cause a stumble."

Raynard took a moment to step away from the books to greet Vail with a handshake and hug. Bringing him over to the table stacked with books, Vail could tell Raynard had been busy for a while.

"Galen told me you would be here." Vail said.

"Anytime a library is near and case is discovered, it is my place to work."

"Speaking of the case. Have you found anything related to these glimpses through time?"

Raynard grabbed one book. A book detailed in the history of Missouri. Flipping through the pages, he told Vail about the history of the state, more so the history of the city. Primarily detailing the Lemp Neighborhood. Vail took note of it, writing details down in a notepad.

"You're writing things down now?" Raynard said to his surprise.

"Yeah. Have any of the witnesses to the case been through the neighborhood?"

"No. this neighborhood the usual when it comes to the paranormal?"

"The ghosts and the like?"

"Yes."

"Very well. I'll keep that in mind once I come back around to the city. Right now, this whole-time case is needed to be solved."

Raynard nodded.

"I did come up with a location related to all the witnesses."

"Where is this place? In the city or outside of it?"

"It's in the city. How else do you expect to have so many witnesses to this case."

"You know how these things go. Strange things always occur outside of the city. Especially cities like this one."

"The Cathedral Basilica of St. Louis. It's over in Central West End region of the city."

"Of all the places I would've thought. The Cathedral was low on my list."

Raynard grinned.

"What were you expecting it to be? The Arch?"

"It fits in this scenario, does it not. Even the Science Center would be a proper place for a time mystery."

Putting the notepad inside his coat pocket, Vail had everything he needed to move on with the case.

"I'll head to the place tonight." Vail said. "Keep my appearance from the public is best."

"I'm sure you will. Although, I'm not certain if the Archbishop will be there."

"In the late hours of the night?"

"Could be possible."

Vail kept that in mind and nodded with a smirk.

Vail shook Raynard's hand and took his leave from the library.

II

INNER BEINGS

Once the night had fallen over St. Louis, Travis Vail arrived at the Cathedral silently. Entering through the front doors with ease seemed a bit unusual for him. However, Vail had entered the cathedral and what threw him off for a moment was the detail of the place. Vail stood inside the main aisle, gazing at the ceiling and the walls. He nodded.

"Nice work they've put in this place."

Vail looked ahead down the aisle and saw what he believed to be a disembodied figure hovering. Moving with speed, Vail ran down the aisle toward the shadow and before he could even get a hand near it, the shadow evaporated with a faint spark of red light. Vail stopped himself as the lights within the cathedral began to flicker. A grin formed upon his face.

"This is what I was expecting." Vail said as he turned around to find himself staring at the figure, fully embodied at the other end of the aisle.

Vail stared at the figure and the details which grabbed him was the attire of the figure. It was dressed just like himself. Black trench coat, white buttoned shirt, black slacks and shoes. It even had a trimmed beard and mustache like Vail.

"Didn't know there were spirits that seemed to like my

fashion." Vail scoffed. "I'm flattered. Now, tell me your name and why you're here."

The figure said nothing. Vail took that as a notion of talk and continued to ask more questions. The figure replied to nothing. Seeing as how talking wasn't moving the conversation along, Vail proceeded to walk down the aisle toward the figure and as he walked, the stench in the air caught him. Stumbling him in his own steps. Shaking his head and covering his nose.

"The hell is that?!"

A grin grew on the figure's shadowed face and Vail realized the stench. His eyes told the story.

"Sulfur. You're a demon, aren't you."

The figure let out a sigh which sounded similar to a growl. Vail continued to walk closer to the figure and after the next step, the figure moved forward into the light for Vail to see. Inching closer, the figure was engulfed in the light and Vail was paused.

"You've got to be shitting me." Vail said with a sigh.

The figure was indeed Vail himself. Yet, with a slight difference. Its face pale and slightly charred. The clothing torn and burnt. The demon showed its fangs toward Vail to Vail's slight humor.

"Ah. Now I get it." Vail said. "You're my demonic counterpart. I've heard of your kind before. I guess everyone has a doppelganger such as yourself. Never thought I would meet my own. Yet, ah the hell with it. What are you doing to this city?"

"I've done nothing." The demon answered. "I've come for you."

"Or you have, eh? Well then. I'm right here."

The demon chuckled as its hands were consumed by fire. The burning of the flames increased the stench of sulfur in the church. Vail fanned his hands to avoid the smell and chuckled under his breath. The demon charged the flames toward Vail in the form of fireballs. Vail ducked quickly to avoid the scorching attack.

"You wanna play." Vail shook his hands, conjuring fire in his own hands. "Let's play."

The two Vails began a battle of wits with fire. Throwing balls of fire toward one another to each own's deflecting. Vail twirled his hands, circling the fire in the air and shoving the circle of fire toward the demon. The demon took the circle for its own use, returning it to Vail in the form of a blast. Vail raised up his hands, conjuring an energy shield, deflecting the blowing flame. The two continued their attacks toward one another as sparks from the flames bounced against the walls of the church.

"You don't give up, I see." Vail chuckled. "We're alike. Aside from the appearance."

Vail gave another spin with his hands, forming a conjunction of the two flames and blasting it into his demonic doppelganger. The blast pushed the demonic Vail through the doors to the outside. Vail rushed out to see the entity and found him laying flat on the ground. A second passed and he rose up. Eyes black as the night sky.

"Typical." Vail smirked.

Lunging to his feet with a snarl, the demonic entity went for a strike until it quickly vanished into a puff of sulfur. Vail stood still. Confused to his doppelganger's disappearance. He sighed.

"Well, that was unexpected."

"Is it?" A echoing voice spoke from behind Vail.

Turning back and looking inside the church, Vail returned inside as he saw at the podium Kamagrauto. The doors behind Vail closed to his dismay as Kamagrauto greeted him. Vail waved slightly before shaking his head.

III
OLD CONFRONTATIONS

"Just who I was expecting." Vail said. "I figure you would be here for something important."

"I came just in time. You know you're not capable of holding back your demonic doppelganger for long."

"I was doing just fine before you arrive. No worries from me."

"But I did come for an important cause."

"I believe you." Vail said while sitting down on the front pew while Kamagrauto remained hovering in front of the podium.

"So, what is the cause you're come for? I hope it concerns myself being in this city. The reason of the matter."

"It does."

"Oh. How good."

"Blessings come in many ways, Spirit-Seeker."

"Yeah. I'm aware. Now, what do you know about what's been happening here?"

"The cause of these time anomalies is the doings of an old adversary of yours."

"Old adversary?" Vail paused. "Well, for certain, I know this isn't the work of Vernon Lance. It's not sinister enough. Can't be Leta. Not her style. I'm not sure who you're referring to."

"You do not remember?"

"Listen, I've come across many malevolent figures. Not all of them retain their names in my mind. Just their attributes of power. Mostly."

"Ugh. I guess you want me to let out the name of the one responsible."

"Might as well. I can still go through with the list of names of the ones I've encountered."

"No need for that. The one responsible for the causes in this city is Balthazar."

Vail paused himself. His eyes shifting back and forth as his mind wandered.

"Balthazar? The same fellow who fled our last encounter some time ago?"

"What other Balthazar do you know of?"

"Not many to be honest with you."

"His workings with the darker forces have provided him a new skill set of shifting time itself. Allowing elements of the past to interfere with the affairs of the present and the distractions through the future."

Vail sighed as he stood up from the pew, gazing around the cathedral.

"Then, what am I waiting for. Where is the fellow now?"

"He's occupied at the Gateway Arch as we speak."

"The Gateway Arch? Why? Ah. Never mind. I get it."

Vail made his way toward the exit and before taking another step, he turned back to Kamagrauto.

"I'm assuming you'll be there?"

"You know me by now, Spirit-Seeker. I'm always around."

After his words touched the air, he vanished from the cathedral to Vail's humorous dismay. Shrugging his shoulders as calm as he is, he exited the cathedral.

IV

ACROSS TIME AND SPACE

While Vail made his arrival at the Arch, he was quickly caught by the flowing energy coming from beneath the Arch. He knew it was Balthazar as he stepped out of his car and saw the hooded figure twirling his arms in the air above his head.

"Every time." Vail said.

Balthazar shrouded his blood-red hood and cloak continued to twirl and spin his arms as his fingers fluttered like electricity in front of the Arch. Vail made his steps quiet to the surprise from the fleeing civilians who sought to avoid the powerful energy. Vail had reached nearly ten feet from Balthazar and stopped.

"Still at this?" Vail yelled through the rushing sound of the energy.

Balthazar's arms froze as his head slowly turned around to gaze toward the Spirit-Seeker. Their eyes touched and a hint of fear grasped the throat of Balthazar.

"Travis Vail?! How? Why?!"

"How am I here? Fully story actually. I heard there had been some time warps happening in this city. Figured it was all caused by some typical supernatural threat. Yet, I've discovered with the help of a friend that it was only you and you alone. To be honest, I'm slightly disappointed."

"This is the problem between you and I."

"What's that?"

"You've never taken me seriously. None of you have."

"Because you only copy what others have done. You've never achieved something on your own to simply call your own."

Balthazar chuckled.

"That is where you're wrong."

"I'm wrong?"

"With the power of this darker force consuming the earth, I have managed to achieve a feat none of you have been capable of doing. I have the power to cross time itself. To bring the past and future to the present. To see the things which have happened and the things yet to come."

"I take it reading history books wasn't enough for you. Much less waiting for the future to happen."

"You don't understand! I can travel to any point in time. See any event and I can alter it to my will. I can make sure you and your allies were never born."

"I've heard that before. Not impressed."

"But, I will let you in on one secret I've uncovered before I kill you."

"Go ahead and speak it. You're getting a little boring."

"Not only can I travel across time. I can travel to other universes. Universes outside of our own. Places yet to be seen. Worlds yet to conquer."

Vail took a moment to step back.

"Universes? I'm not sure you want to trouble them, Balthazar. You may come across someone who won't take you as lightly as I am right now."

Balthazar's hands flashed and was consumed by the same glowing white energy from the Arch. A grin formed upon his face as even his eyes shined like the energy.

"I guess I'll have to show you."

Balthazar stretched his arms, blasting the energy toward Vail as he jumped out of its path. Down on the ground, Vail rose up and conjured up several balls of fire and threw them into Balthazar's chest, shoving him back near the Arch as the energy continued to pour through. The attacks between the two continued until Vail looked up near the Arch and saw Kamagrauto.

"Knock him in." Kamagrauto yelled.

Vail looked as Balthazar wiped the flames from his clothing and his closeness toward the Arch. Shrugging his shoulders, Vail ran and speared Balthazar as the two entered the energy, quickly transporting themselves through a wormhole of stars, water, fire, and earth. Flowing through the wormhole, Balthazar continued his attacks as Vail deflected the energy blast with a shield of his own making. Vail retailed with a blast of his own, striking Balthazar as they both fell into an opening of the wormhole and landing in a desert.

"The hell are we?" Vail questioned.

Gazing around the desert, Vail turned around to see the Pyramids of Giza. However, they were not worn-out as they shined brightly with their white coating as the sun rose over them.

"We're in the past." Vail said to himself. "We're in Ancient Egypt."

Hearing the rush of dirt behind him, Vail turned as he saw Balthazar standing up from the fall. his eyes wandered around the desert during the clear day and he saw the glinting light of the pyramids. He turned toward Vail as he pointed at the pyramids.

"See! I told you! I have the power!"

"We can't stay here. We're going back."

"I'm going back. You will remain here!"

Another blast came from Balthazar's hands with Vail deflecting them once again. The energy from the Arch bolted from sky as Balthazar went to run for it. Vail followed him as he began to hear the sound of horses from behind. Turning to get a gaze,

Vail saw the armies of the Pharaoh rushing toward them.

"Not what I was expecting this day to go."

Balthazar jumped into the bolting energy as Vail latched his hand onto Balthazar's cloak and the two went back into the wormhole just as the Egyptian army came near to them. Moving at great speed in the wormhole, the two continued their battle with Balthazar's energy blasts and Vail's fireballs. A second hole opened in the wormhole, causing them to fall into another set of sand. This time, Vail raised his head to find himself staring into the face of a lion. The lion lunged toward Vail, only for him to realize the lion was caged. The noise of a crowd shocked them as both Vail and Balthazar looked around.

"Where did you send us?" Balthazar said.

"You're the one with the traveling. But, I know where we are."

The crowds cheered and roared with excitement as Vail and Balthazar found themselves in the times of Ancient Rome, standing in the middle of the Roman Coliseum. The gates within the coliseum opened as armies of gladiators entered. Vail's hands conjured more flames as Balthazar's hands continued to glow. The gladiators looked at them, seeing their apparel and mocked as their hands gripped their swords and spears.

"You know what we have to do." Vail said.

"I'm not getting what you're saying."

"Until the beam comes down again, we'll have to work together to survive."

"They're nothing but brute beasts. What can a sword do against the might of magic."

The gladiators rushed into the fight against Vail and Balthazar. Vail deflected the swipes of their blades and retaliated with a flaming sword of his own. Formed from the flames on his hands. The embers shared from the clashing of the swords as Balthazar levitated himself above the battlefield, raining down energy blasts from his hands across the sands. The blasts knocked down the gladiators as the cages opened, releasing the lions. Vail looked as he saw the beasts charging toward them and a shockwave emitted from the sky, grabbing everyone's attention. The beam had returned and both Vail and Balthazar jumped in before the lions had them in their grasps. Moving around back through the wormhole, Vail could only wonder where they would end up next. Hoping they'll return to the Arch, the opening returned as the fell through, crashing on a road. Regaining themselves from the fall, Vail looked up, finding them both in a city lit by neon lighting. The streets were concrete just as the rain began to fall.

"What is this place?" Balthazar questioned. "The energy here is different."

Vail watched as the bystanders stared at them as if they were foreigners. Looking at the moving signs on the buildings describing the merging of humans and machines. One board presented a phrase Vail was not familiar with.

"For the Man-God?"

"We don't tolerate strangers in our city." A bystander yelled.

"Stranger?" Vail said. "What the hell is that?"

The beam returned and they entered just as the bystanders began to move away in fear of someone else entering their city. All Vail could see before the beam took him and Balthazar was the silhouette of a hat and coat. Through the beam they went once more, now they fell onto a dead landscape. Nothing growing. Only the dirt remained. The sky above them shrouded in a dark red as if under a tent. The moon was red and the sun was unable to be found.

"I know where we are now." Vail said. "We're in the future."

"What future?" Balthazar questioned.

"The end of the world as we know it."

Around them, they could hear a battle taking place as lighting fell from the sky. Vail ran to see the battle and discovered it was covered with all the armies of the world and villains. Even some of the heroes were there in the fight. Many he did not recognize. There were others on the battlefield that was strange to Vail and Balthazar. They wielded swords of embedding light. A crack of thunder roamed over above them in the sky as the clouds began to open to the sound of a trumpet gathering everyone's attention. Some of the heroes had vanished while the armies and villains remained. Their eyes locked on the clouds and their weapons aimed.

"I know what this is." Vail said. "We're standing on the battlefields of Megiddo and He has returned."

Before Vail could see who was coming through the clouds, the beam returned and gathered him and Balthazar as a bright flash of light poured from the clouds, covering the ground in a white shine in which the armies and villains were blinded by the sight. Through the wormhole once more and with a flash, Vail and Balthazar found themselves being tossed out of the Arch. Looking around as they found themselves back in St. Louis, Vail looked up, seeing Kamagratuto still in his place.

"Balthazar, shut this down!"

"I cannot. It is my purpose."

Vail shook his head with a low sigh, reaching into his jacket pocket taking out his book. Turning the page as Balthazar went to return to his twirling spell, Vail began to recite out of the book as the Arch's billowing energy slowly came to an end. Balthazar yelled as the energy evaporated from the Arch and his hands became still. There was no energy within him. Not even sparks emitted from his hands.

"What have you done to me?!"

"I only stopped you before you caused greater damage. Leave this city, Balthazar. Go find something productive outside the realm of magic."

"I will not be defeated this day!"

Balthazar went to strike Vail, yet was blocked by Kamagrauto who appeared in between the two men. Balthazar looked in terror at the lieutenant demon and teleported himself from the site. Vail was not amused.

"He does that every time."

"It appears it is over." Kamagrauto spoke.

"Yeah. Well, that ends the case for today."

The next day, Vail closed the case on the mysteries of St. Louis as it was all the workings of Balthazar. Leaving the city, Vail received a phone call from Gabriel Abraham. Detailing some strange events taking place across the world. The news of a darker presence had made itself known. This is a case Vail knew for certain needed his expertise.

THE DEVILHUNTER: COVEN OF DREAD

I

A NIGHT OUT

Walking through the suburban home in the Pleasant Plains neighborhood of Washington D.C. were Evan, Andrea, and Abraham. Each of them carried flashlights as the home's electricity was cut due to the decreased living it had received over the past three weeks. News had spread throughout the neighborhood of the home being haunted by a ghostly figure dressed in pirate-garb and wielding a hook in its right hand.

"So, did either of you learn more about this haunting?" Abraham asked.

"Only what the surrounding neighbors have told the authorities." Evan replied. "Nothing more."

"Any about the ghost?"

"Besides the fact he's carrying a hook?" Andrea joked. "Not sure we've learned anything else other than that."

"This ghost is not something entirely new. It's an urban legend that's been around for a very long time. Just not in this region."

"What are you saying?" Evan wondered. "Did this ghost travel all the way here for a reason?"

"It would only make sense of that. Meaning something is wrong."

Walking through the home, they come toward the hallway with three doors in their path. Abraham takes one as Evan and Andrea take the other two. In the first door where Abraham entered, he only found himself within a bedroom. One bed, a TV near the wall, and a shelf where a few books were standing. Abraham took a closer look at the books, seeing them to be books on the subjects of the supernatural. He scoffed. In the other rooms, Evan and Andrea only saw beds, shelves, and desks. Each of them stepping out of the rooms at the same time. Seeing each other in the hall.

"Nothing." Evan said.

"Same here." Andrea spoke.

"The books in that room, they were on the subjects f the supernatural."

"Then, the people who lived here were aware of it. This makes it more intriguing."

"Don't get all into it." Abraham said. "Right now, we need to find this ghost and end this."

While discussing other options to search the home, the floors creaked, causing them to pause. The flashlights moving through the hallway back to the entrance where the creaking continued. Abraham took a step forward with Evan and Andrea behind him. The creaking became footsteps. Coming from the front door. They prepared themselves as the footsteps grew with every creak. The sound of them ringed in Abraham's mind.

"Those are boots." He whispered.

Abraham stood against eh wall with his flashlight aimed toward the hallway where they entered. Telling Evan and Andrea to do the same as the three flashlights lit up the hallway entry point where they saw a figure standing with the last step. Cloaked in what looked to be a long raincoat and hat. His face shrouded from their sight. To them, he had no face. Only darkness. Abraham glanced down toward the shadow's hand, seeing the glinting hook.

"It's him."

The Hookman moved toward them with his hand raised and the hook came down, Abraham dodged the attack, stepping back as Evan and Andrea made a run for it down the hallway. Abraham dodged the swiping from the hook as the Hookman grunted in anger.

"Whomever you are," Abraham yelled. "You do not belong here!"

The Hookman did not respond and continued his attack. Evan and Andrea ran into one of the rooms and shut the door. Hearing only he commotion from the outside as Abraham's voice echoed with every slash from the hook.

"We need to help him." Evan said.

"But how?"

Outside in the hallway, Abraham moved to the other end as the Hookman continued to slash toward him. Evan and Andrea come out of the room, standing behind the Hookman and are paused in place. The Hookman stopped his attack and turned around to face them. Abraham seen the fear in their eyes as the Hookman had them in the right spot.

"Andrea!" Abraham yelled. "Raise up your arms!"

"What? Why?!"

"Just do it."

Confusion ran through her mind as she lifted her arms. The Hookman saw her and began to lower the hook. Evan stood in confusion to what was happening. Abraham nodded quietly as he told them to come around him. Taking small steps, they walked past the Hookman without him attacking. Reaching the end of the hallway, the two went for the front door as Abraham chose to deal with the Hookman himself. Once the sound of te front door shut, the Hookman regained himself and went to strike at Abraham once more. Only this time, Abraham stretched forth his hand and the Hookman paused.

"This is not your home. This is not your place. I command you with all that is benevolent that you return to your resting place and ever step foot in this home or on this land again!"

The Hookman glanced at his right hand, seeing it evaporating into nothing. His left arm followed and his legs. Before he completely vanished, a word whispered from his shrouded face. A word that Abraham caught in his ears just as the Hookman disappeared.

While Evan and Andrea waited outside by the car for Abraham to exit the home, they watched the streets for any of the neighbors. In case they were intrigued by what might happened. To their surprise, no neighbors were standing outside of the home. Evan took it as their sign of fear. Abraham exited the home and walked down the steps toward the car.

"Is he gone?" Evan asked.

"He's gone."

"Then we've done our job." Andrea said. "The home is secure."

"It is." Abraham said quietly.

"Abraham." Evan said. "What is it?"

"Before the Hookman vanished, he whispered a word to me. It's not what I've read from his previous encounters across the country."

"What did he say?"

"Coven. He said the word Coven."

"Coven? I'm not sure what that could mean."

"I didn't read about any Coven in the sightings folder." Andrea said. "Does that mean something else is going on that we don't know about?"

"I have an idea." Abraham replied. "This case is complete. However, we have work to do."

II

WITCH HUNT

The following morning, Abraham, Evan, and Andrea immediately went into the study concerning the Hookman's echoed word. Through their continuous studying throughout the day, Evan opened one of the books and discovered a history involving covens throughout the regions of Delaware. Most was during the time of the Witch Trials. Abraham grabbed the large and worn-out book, reading the details.

"I know this spot."

"You do?" Andrea said. "Where is it?"

"Not far from here." Abraham nodded. "I think I have an idea as to what the Hookman meant."

"So, what's the plan?" Evan questioned. "The three of us head out to this place and uncover the mystery?"

"No. I'll head to the spot. You two," Abraham said, while gazing toward the image of a castle. "Go to this place."

Evan and Andrea looked at the image in the book. Seeing the old castle.

"You want us to go to this castle?" Andrea asked.

"Yes. Figured it would suit you two. I'll go and check out this forest."

Abraham closed the book, leaving it on the table. Once they headed out toward their destinations, Abraham was focused on learning more about the Coven. While heading out toward the location he found as familiar, he arrived. Seeing an old field with an old home. Stepping out of his car while his eyes were set on the home, an eerie feeling made itself present before Abraham.

"Who's here?" He asked.

The front door of the home bolted open as if wind had entered. Yet there was no wind. Not even a small blow. Abraham's eyes focused on the door as he could make out the shadow of a figure. One of a feminine nature.

"Step out of the house." Abraham said. "Do it now."

The shadow paused to Abraham's displeasure. Reaching into his pocket, he raised up a gun and held it toward the shadow. Demanding for whomever it may be to make themselves known to him. The shrouded figure stepped from the door to Abraham's sigh, yet caution.

"You?" Abraham uttered.

"I know. You're surprised to see me again."

"I am. Sierra the Succubus. Tell me, why are you here and why dwell inside this home?"

"Because it is mine."

"I'm not here to fight."

"Then why are you here, Devilhunter?"

"I've heard rumors of a coven working in the area. I'm searching for them. According to my research, they've been through this area. Somehow, I've only found you."

"A coven? You mean a group of witches."

"What else would a coven be? Have you seen them?"

"Have I seen any witches?"

"Yes."

"No. I haven't. but, if I did, I would most likely throw them off my property. I have no taste for witches."

Abraham nodded as his still held up the gun. Sierra sighed with annoyance at the sight. Commanding him to lower the weapon. Abraham was not subtle in his place facing her. He knew what she was capable of.

"Look, there are no witches here. So, I suggest you take your leave."

"I would. However, I cannot let you linger here for much longer. When this case of the coven is done, I will be coming back here to kick you out as well."

Sierra shrugged her shoulders with a growing grin on her face. She welcomed the challenge to come as Abraham turned and took his leave.

Elsewhere, Evan and Andrea drove through the wilderness of the land in search of the supposed castle ruins. Andrea stared out the window towards the land, seeing nothing but trees. She sighed as there was no trace of a castle.

"Don't give up just yet." Evan said.

"I'm not giving up. It's just, you can't see much through the woods. Would be easier if there was a clearer view."

Looking back outside toward the trees, Andréa spotted something within the wilderness. A glowing of some sort. She pointed with a yelp screeching from his mouth, startling Evan.

"What's on with you?!"

"There! There's something in the woods. A glow."

"You're sure its not someone walking around with a flashlight or something? You know like a ranger?"

"If rangers these days carry red flashlights, perhaps. However, I don't believe they have red flashlights, do they?"

"No. They do not."

Evan moved the car to the side of the road and stopped.

"We'll have to go on foot."

"In the dark?" Andrea questioned.

"We have no choice. Besides, we have flashlights of our own."

"Where?"

"The glove box." Evan pointed.

Andrea nodded with a smile as she opened the glove box, taking out the flashlights. They exited the vehicle and headed into the wilderness in the middle of the night. No fear on Evan while Andrea was slightly shaken by the darkness. Stepping on the downed leaves and limbs sent a chill down her spine to Evan's humor.

"Did I just hear a giggle?" She said.

"Maybe. Maybe not."

Seeing the traces of red glint in the distance, they made a run for it with Evan first. Andrea paused as she saw him running toward the light. From there, she followed him until she noticed he came to a sudden stop. Reaching him, she saw what Evan was staring at.

"What are those?" She questioned.

"They're sigils. Sigils aren't just placed out in the middle of nowhere on their own."

"No they're not." Andrea raised her head from the sigils and pointed. "You see that?"

Evan glanced upward, looking in Andrea's direction. He waved the flashlight.

"What is it?"

Looking ahead of them, they could only stare at the tall bricked tower. Moving to the side to gain a better look and waving their flashlights around the see the fullness through the darkness, they found themselves the ruins of a castle.

"I'm confused about this." Evan said.

"How come?"

"Because I'm not too sure there were any castles in this region of the country. By the look of the stonework, this castle must've been built during the early 15th century."

"You're serious?"

"I am." Evan sighed. "We should go ahead and tell Gabriel about all of this. Especially the sigils."

"The Coven is using the runs as a base."

"You just realized that."

"In a way."

III

WELCOME TO OUR HOME

Evan and Andrea returned to the Center just in time as Abraham sat inside, going through a grimier with the pages detailed in combating a succubus. Once Evan and Andrea stepped foot into the office, Abraham closed the book and gave them his attention.

"What have you found?"

"We found a castle." Andrea said. "The ruins of one at least."

"Castle ruins?" Abraham said. "This close to D.C.?"

"I know. I found it strange myself. I don't believe there were any castles in this area of North America. The stonework dates back to the 1400s."

"Interesting. Did you find anything else? Anything related to this supposed coven?"

"We found sigils."

"Sigils?"

"Glowing sigils." Andrea said. "They were surrounding the castle ruins."

Abraham nodded with a grunt as he slid the grimoire aside. He prepped himself and gathered his gear, heading for the door.

"Where are you going?" Evan asked.

"To the ruins. Aren't you coming along or do you want to stay here?"

Evan and Andrea looked at each other. One with a grin. The other only a slant of a smile. Either way, they agreed and headed out with Abraham back to the ruins.

Upon their arrival, Evan immediately noticed the color change of the sigils. Abraham did not hesitate as he went into the ruins. Walking in to only the echo of his own footsteps, he saw a pedestal standing by itself, surrounding with figs and violet flowers. Evan and Andrea followed him and came to a stop at the sight of the pedestal.

"What's that?"

"That is what witches use, Evan." Abraham said. "You two found the spot. Good work."

"Oh, it's nothing." Andrea said. "Rather like a quick work, wasn't it Evan?"

"You did see the sigils' glow. So, that leaves the following question."

"Where is the coven?" Abraham said.

On the outside of the ruins, a sudden burst of wind rose from the ground. Billowing around the castle. Abraham stepped further in as he was only three feet from the pedestal, Evan and Andrea stood beside him, prepared for whatever was coming their way. Abraham was not caught off guard. He knew the source of the sudden wind.

"They're here." Abraham said.

"Who's here?" Evan said. "I don't see anybody."

The wind's strength decreased as a red mist rose from the dirt of the fields, covering the ruins in a shadow of its own making. Through the mist appeared three figures. emerging through the blood-red covering were three women, clothed in robes of scarlet and purple. Their eyes shadowed by darkness.

"Them." Abraham said.

IV

DO WITCHES FEAR FIRE?

Abraham stood prepared to face the three women. He knew they were of the Coven. Witches throughout the darkness. Unseen by the population. The witch in the middle grinned at Abraham with a wink. Evan and Andrea were unsure as to what move to make while Abraham had his right hand in his pocket as he left was out and open.

"We were waiting for you to discover us."

"Discover you?" Abraham said. "You knew we were searching for you?"

"Of course. Is it not the duty of a witch to keep watch and preserve her coven against any foe natural or supernatural?"

"Perhaps. I'm going to give you this moment to walk away and leave this region of the country. Return to your place of origin at once."

The witches laughed at Abraham's command. Leaving him standing silent. Evan and Andrea stepped forward with propositions of their own. Evan suggested they go to a neighboring city while Andrea presented the idea of the coven working on the opposite side of D.C. Each one Abraham answered with a stone-faced look.

"We are not leaving." The witch said. "This is our place of

dominion. We shall rule this land."

"No. you will not." Abraham answered coldly. "You will leave at once. That is my final answer."

The witches boldly stood against Abraham as the red mist continued to move around the ruins. Evan and Andrea each took steps back while Abraham stepped forward. No fear in him as he faced the witches. The three witches giggled as they glanced to one another.

"You leave us no other option, Devilhunter. This night shall be your last."

"My last? You're sure it isn't yours?"

Abraham stretched his hands upward and from the stone walls blasted pillars of fire. Startling the witches. Using their magic, the witches retaliated against the flames as Abraham held them still. His hands shaking from the strength while Evan and Andrea watched in amazement.

"How are you doing this?" Evan asked.

"I've learned a thing or two. Studying helps out a lot."

The flames move from the walls surrounding the witches onto the ground. Creating a wall between Abraham, Evan, Andrea, and the witches. Through eh searing flames, the center witch glared toward Abraham. He could sense the darkness within her. She quickly stretched her hand toward him.

"You are a clever one, Devilhunter! Yet, this is not our final stand!"

"Leave." Abraham said. "Never come back. Or be consumed."

The witches levitated from the ground, attempting to bolt throughout the flames. With each attempt, one of the pillars of fire increased in height and strength. Their screeches revealed their anger to the point the center witch called for a retreat and they vanished through the mist. The pillars decreased as the mist evaporated. Only the stillness of the air remained with small embers billowing from the burnt grass.

"Is, is that all?" Evan questioned.

"For now." Abraham answered. "They'll be back. Stronger and with more witches on their side."

"So, what's next on the agenda?" Andrea wondered.

"We cleansed this place of their residue. Remove their sigils and anything related to their coven. That way they can never return here. A place secured from their wickedness."

The three managed to cleanse the land of the coven's powers. The sigils were removed by Andrea, who stretched them from the stone. Abraham became a séance ritual across the land from the ruins to the woods to the road. Evan helped Andrea with the burning of the remaining sigils. They returned to the Center once the work was completed and rested.

The following day as they awoke, they received a visitor at the door. Abraham arose and answered the knocking, only to see an old friend standing by.

"Ah, Travis Vail. Nice to see you once again."

"This is becoming a habit, isn't it." Vail grinned.

"Why have you come? Something happened?"

"A lot and I hope you're ready. And your colleagues."

"Is it that bad?"

"Much worse I'm afraid."

THE MAN CALLED FABLE: MAGIC AND SEEK

I

VISITORS

Taking a stroll through the streets of Manchester, The Man Called Fable walked past civilians. Some were aware of his existence. Others perceived him as a stranger to the city. Fable didn't mind. After all the things which have happened previously to his current walk, Fable didn't care of the opinions of those outside of his circle. Be them human or magical. Fable walked with a smile on face. Something familiar to his demeanor. As he walked, a gust of wind blew in his direction. Taking his focus from the day. He stopped and glanced around as the wind began to grow stronger. The quick sound of a boom emitted behind him, startling the civilians and as Fable turned, he saw Pandora. Behind her was a gateway.

"Again?" Fable said.

"I would've have come unless there was something urgent."

"I know. I know. What is it this time?"

"The Hidden Four demand your presence."

"At the homestead?"

Pandora raised her hand, gesturing toward the portal. Fable sighed as he approached the portal and entered. Within Fable found himself in the center of a courtroom. Sitting before him in the chairs were the Hidden Four. Their eyes unseen, yet their gaze could be felt upon Fable's spirit. Pandora entered behind him as the portal closed. Fable greeted the Four as before. With grins and no concern.

"Kurt Wesker, we would not have summoned you if it was not of importance."

"I am aware. Trust me."

"But, what has come up will need your assistance in the matter."

"And this matter is?"

"Ananse." One of the Four answered.

"Ananse? You're referring to the Spider God from Africa?"

"Yes." Pandora said. "He's on the loose and we need you to find him."

Fable sighed with a shake of the head. He glanced toward the Four before looking at Pandora.

"And where am I supposed to go to track him down? You do have some sort of evidence on his recent activities?"

"He was last spotted moving through the cities in Africa. That is your next stop."

Fable sighed.

"Sure. Sure. I'll find this Ananse."

II
THE SPIDER GOD

    Through the rift, Fable opened a portal to Ethiopia. Walking through the city of Addis Ababa, Fable sensed a strangeness in the air. Even within the people. They knew something and were keen to keep it quiet. Fable didn't bother the civilians during his walk. Pausing for a moment, Fable took out a card, reading it. The card spoke of a Shaman who had insight knowledge to Ananse.
    "All I have to do now is find this shaman."
    A whisper moved past Fable's ears like a buzzing fly. He knew it was no simple whisper as it called to him by name. commanding him to follow it. Fable proceeded and followed the whisper, leading him to a small building. Renovation had yet to be complete, but the whisper had come from within. Fable entered the doors and inside of the building was only a man sitting on the floor, surrounded by candles and bones. Fable chuckled.
    "You're him. You're the shaman I'm looking for."
    "I was expecting your arrival." The Shaman said. "You've come here seeking to find the Spider God, no?"
    "That is why I've come. I need to find him and get him to cease what he's doing."
    "And what is he doing that causes concern?"
    "His actions. His motives. He's going around the world and

through the Rift causing trouble."

"And is this what you believe or what your peers believe?'

Fable took notice. He grinned.

"Fair point. I've come only to find him. The others are seeking to bring him in. They're the ones with the problem. Not I."

"So, I see."

"Will you help me?"

"I will. Please sit."

Fable took a seat in front of the Shaman on the floor as he continued to blow incense.

"The Spider God knows you've been sent to find him."

"How do you know this?"

"Because I know a lot about him. His history. His works. His motives. The Spider God is well across these lands."

"I just need to find him. That's all."

"You don't find him. He finds you."

Fable sighed.

"By the way, you've never told me your name." Fable said.

"Shaman Badru. That is my name in this life."

"Good to speak with you, Shaman Badru."

Fable stood up from the floor and took his leave. Seeing as he couldn't find Ananse on his own, he would wait for the Spider God to make himself known.

III

A GAME OF MAGIC AND SEEK

Fable waited in Shaman Badru's place for hours, seeing if Ananse would appear. Within hours, there was nothing. No sign of the Spider God. Fable saw this as a waste of time and took his leave from Badru's place. Walking outside, Fable went to search for a good place to open a portal. He was finished with this mission and look to tell the Hidden Four all he could do. Coming into an alleyway, Fable looked back and forth, seeing no one other than himself in the alley.

"Good place as any."

Fable went to open a portal into the Rift, yet behind him came a peculiar voice. Fable stopped the portal's opening and turned around to see a man dressed in a burgundy suit. His hair was black as coal and his eyes glowed during the day. Fable watched him and looked closer. He grinned.

"You've finally shown yourself." Fable said. "Why now?"

"Why now? You ask. It's very simple. I needed to see if you had the enduring substance to hold on. I needed to truly know you were seeking me and it seems you were."

"I'm only here on a mission. The Hidden Four have requested you come to them to answer some questions."

Ananse chuckled.

"What does the hooded ones want with a guy like me? What have I done to cause them such dismay?"

"Beats me. I'm only here to bring you in. Since you're here, we can go ahead and finish this now."

Ananse nodded with a grin. He clapped his hands and rubbed them together.

"Very well. I'll have a chat with the hooded ones. Open the portal, Englishman."

Fable, looking confused, opened the portal into the Rift and he and Ananse entered. Sanding before the Hidden Four, Ananse approached them as close as possible. Pandora was also inside as she saw Ananse walking freely in the room.

"You found him."

"Actually, he found me. Chose to come here as well. He wanted to talk to them."

"About what?"

"Didn't tell me. None of my concern. Now, I will return to Manchester."

"You've done well, Kurt Wesker." One of the Four said.

"Thank you," Fable waved.

The Rift opened into Manchester as Fable stepped forward and returned to the city. Some days after, words had spread throughout the city of a darker power being noticed by several civilians. Even the magical beings have gone into hiding to avoid the power. This intrigued Fable and he began to look into the new unseen mystery.

DOCTOR FORTUNE: SPIRITUAL GODFARE

I
VISITORS OF A KIND

Within the Citadel of Enchantment, Doctor Fortune continued his tutoring with Tom Bradley in the form of the mystic arts. Huang was inside one of the studies, researching more work into the mystics. Fortune and Bradley trained with mystic shields, swords, spears, and fire.

"How much goes into this completely?" Tom asked.

"Everything." Fortune answered. "Everything you learn is an aid to the cause."

The training continued until the sound of a rushing, mighty wind began to catch their attention. Fortune paused the training as he looked outside the windows. Hearing the wind, yet, seeing nothing pass them by. Huang came out from the study as he could hear the same thing. He glanced over to Fortune and Fortune to him.

"I see nothing outside." Fortune said.

"It's something." Huang said. "We need to find out immediately."

Through the wind, the sounds of snarls could be heard and Fortune knew they were under attack. Huang was ready for the fight and Tom was prepared as best as possible. The three stood together as the wind began to slam against the front doors. The snarls had followed the banging. The noises ceased, Fortune however was not to be caught off guard as his hands and forearms began to glow a violet light from the mystic powers.

"Don't keep us waiting any longer."

The front doors shattered open as a horde of robotic beings entered the Citadel. Fortune blasted several of them with his mystic fire blasts. Huang followed suit with energy beams and weaponry of his own. Tom conjured a mystic staff and fought against the rushing robots.

"What is all of this?" Huang asked. "Octagon again?"

"This isn't Octagon." Fortune said. "This is someone else."

At the entrance to the Citadel, behind the horde of robots stood a figure. While taking down the robots, Fortune looked and caught a glimpse of the figure. He knew it wasn't Octagon or anyone he's come into conflict with. This was something new. Something different for the Supreme Enchanter.

"Huang, Tom. Handle the robots."

"Where are you going?" Huang asked as he slashed the head of one robot.

"I'm going to see who's standing at my door."

Fortune flew through the robots as he made his way toward the entrance. Stopping near the broken doors, Fortune saw the figure in full. The two stared each other down. Neither have met the other.

"Who are you supposed to be?" Fortune questioned.

"Stroh. King Stroh. The Conqueror."

"A conqueror?" Fortune said. "I've never heard of you before."

"I've been to this world before. My first venture was thwarted by the ones this world call heroes."

Fortune nodded. He knew this was the figure The Resistance defeated sometime before the Octagon incident. Stroh stood still. His hands behind his back. His face emotionless aside from his glowing emerald eyes.

"Well, you've come to the wrong place." Fortune said. "Best you take what's left of your little army and leave my Citadel before you end up like them."

"I will leave when I choose to."

Fortune clapped his hands as the mystic powers brightened. Stroh was not bothered.

"Return to your own world at once. I will not ask again."

"Keep on asking, Enchanter." A voice uttered from the outside. "He will not be moved."

Fortune looked out as he heard the vice. Levitating down to the ground beside Stroh was Celd. Fortune knew he would return, yet not with a new ally.

"You're back." Fortune said.

"I am and for a very, very good reason."

"Nothing is good when it comes to you."

"Depends on who's side your own. Such like Stroh here. The two of us came to an agreement and you're in our way."

"I'm in your way? Seems like I'm a threat to your works."

"You are." Celd said. "I have no need to look down upon it. You're the Supreme Enchanter. There is no other."

"Best you both leave this place or you'll end up like the robots you see on the floor."

"Figured you'll say something of the sort."

Celd raised his hands and a large blast of energy emitted from the palms. Striking Fortune, Tom, and Huang. Even the remaining robots fell from the blast. The light went down as they saw everyone on the ground. Stroh stood quiet as Celd laughed at the scene.

"We've done our job here. On to the next location."

Celd flew off into the air as Stroh disappeared through the means of technological teleportation. Through the debris, Fortune arose with anger in his being. Tom was also standing as he helped

Huang to his feet.

"Who were those guys?" Tom asked.

"One was Celd, a powerful entity in the mystic arts." Fortune answered. "The other called himself King Stroh The Conqueror."

"What do they want?" Huang asked.

"To takeover. It's always in their plans."

"Then we have to stop them." Tom said. "Somehow."

"I have an idea." Fortune said. "But, I'm not sure he'll help us in this quest."

II

A JUDGMENT CALL

Through the opening portal of mystic energy, Fortune, Huang, and Tom stepped out and as the portal closed, they looked ahead to the horizon to see Palace Judge. The three were standing in the city of Judgedath within the Kingdom of Centro. A place all too familiar with them. The air was still, yet a presence surrounded them. Not one of the spiritual nature, yet of a natural sort. They walked toward the palace and immediately saw several judgedroids standing at the gate of the palace.

"You think they'll attack?" Tom asked.

"No." Fortune said. "I've already sent the message that we're here."

Approaching the gate, the judgedroids stared at the three sorcerers for about a minute. Afterwards, they stepped aside as the gate opened. Entering the palace, they arrived at the throne room. Stopping in their steps, they looked and saw Sinister Judge himself sitting. Once Judge's eyes caught their arrival, he arose from the seat and quickly attacked without notice. The three sorcerers moved aside as Judge continued to fire mystical blasts toward them. Fortune deflected the blasts with shields of his own. Huang followed with fire blasts, only for Judge to take them and mix them with his own attacks.

"Enough!" Fortune yelled as one of Judge's blasts pushed against one of his shields.

Judge stopped the attacks and stared at Fortune. His eyes didn't even ponder Huang and Tom. He turned around and returned to the throne and sat down. His eyes still on Fortune as the Supreme Enchanter stepped forward with Judge at his front and Huang and Tom behind him.

"You sent word of your arrival." Judge said. "You've entered my palace with no battle. Now, you stand before Judge. Tell me, why have you chosen to come to my kingdom this day?"

"The Citadel was attacked by two individuals. Celd and the other called himself King Stroh The Conqueror. Something is taking place and we can't stop them alone."

"You've come here with a hope I would align with you against the two attackers?"

"I assumed you would. Because they're coming for everyone who delves into the mystic arts. That includes you, Judge."

"Let them try to attack my kingdom. I do not fear this Celd you speak of nor this Conqueror. There is only one conqueror and it is Judge."

Fortune looked up to the ceiling and sensed a strangeness in the air. He felt the same source back at the Citadel. Judge knew what he was doing and nodded.

"Yes. You sense it as well."

"What is it?"

"There's a darker power moving throughout the world. Something is happening outside of our gazes and it is only a matter of time before it reveals itself to us all. I'm doing my part in uncovering such trouble."

"And what have you found so far?"

"Human work is at play. Delving in such arts that will only bring forth destruction. I don't know who they are, but I will find out soon."

"Until then, I need your help in defeating Celd and this King Stroh. Together, we can take them down."

Judge thought and nodded.

"Very well, Enchanter. I will join you in this quest. Only to make sure these two attackers do not cause a threat to my kingdom."

Huang approached Fortune while glaring toward Judge.

"So, will he help us?"

"Appears to be the case."

"Now, what's next?" Tom asked.

"We're not enough. I need to go and find one more sorcerer to join us."

"Go and find this sorcerer." Judge said. "Once you do, return here in that we must plan out our actions accordingly."

Fortune nodded.

"It will not take me too long." Fortune disappeared through a portal.

Huang and Tom stood in the throne room as Judge sat and remained silent. His eyes not even touching the two sorcerers.

Elsewhere, Fortune appeared in front of a home. He stepped toward the door and knocked. After the third knock, the door opened to reveal Morhana. She saw Fortune and he greeted her with a smile. She sighed.

"What are you doing here?"

"I wouldn't have come if it wasn't serious. Completely serious is a better term for it."

Morhana allowed Fortune into her home. Inside, Fortune sat down in the living room with Morhana.

"So, what is happening?" Morhana said.

"The Citadel was attacked by Celd and another being who called himself King Stroh The Conqueror."

"Is Huang and Tom well?"

"They're fine. They're currently at Palace Judge awaiting my return."

"Hold on. I'm sorry. Palace Judge? You mean the dwelling place of Sinister Judge?"

"I need his help on this. Celd and this Conqueror will be making their rounds on every sorcerer. That includes Judge and yourself."

"So I see."

"Now you understand why I've come to you. I need your help on this one. These two beings. Celd I know from experience. However, this Conqueror, I do not know his motives nor what he can truly do."

Morhana nodded as she pondered the idea of joining Fortune in this battle.

"Usually you would join in without haste. Ready for the battle ahead. What is it this time?"

"Judge. You can't trust him."

"I didn't say I trusted him. We had our bouts in the past and I'm certain we will in the future. But right now, we're on the same side against these powerful forces. Morhana, will you help us in taking them down before they bring much trouble to the world."

Morhana stood up from the couch and walked toward the window, gazing out to the city ahead.

"What do you say?" Fortune asked.

"Ugh. As much as I refuse to stand next to Judge, this is bigger than him whether he knows it or not. But, the world is at stake for help and we can't allow Celd and this Conqueror to roam the earth to do their trouble. So, Donald, I will assist you in this fight."

Fortune stood up from his seat.

"Thank you. Because we'll need it."

"What now?"

"Now, we return to Palace Judge and figure out a plan to find Celd and King Stroh before they find us."

"Wait. We're going to Judge's Palace? Why not the Citadel to make up a plan?"

"Because Judge is involved in this. He's already in one place. Making the plan there is a good enough situation."

"If you say so." Morhana sighed. "Let's get this over with then."

III

SERVANTS OF WAR

The portal opened in the throne room as Fortune and Morhana stepped through. Morhana saw Huang and Tom as she greeted them with hugs. She turned around and saw Judge sitting on the throne and rolled her eyes. Judge chuckled under his breath.

"Have you found everyone you need, Enchanter?"

"I have. Now we can come up with a plan to stop them."

Judge waved his hands and in the middle of the throne room floor arose a table. Fortune stepped back as the table formed through the means of technology and magic. He was impressed with Judge's choice of use. Fortune used the table to conjure a detailed map of magical essence through the earth's atmosphere. On the map were traces that led to Celd and King Stroh.

"Where can we find them?" Morhana asked.

"We follow the trails." Fortune answered. "Two trails. We each could split up and confront them without their knowing."

"Or we could face them now." Judge said. "There is no more waiting."

"Why are you so keen on rushing into battle?" Morhana asked.

"I am not rushing. There's no need in finding them."

"Why not?" Fortune asked.

"Because they're already here." Judge said as a loud boom exploded outside the palace.

Huang and Tom ran to the outside to see three judgedroids being decimated by the Followers of Stroh. Up in the sky hovered Stroh himself as Celd appeared from a portal above. Judge stretched forth his hand and an arsenal of judgedroids appeared and clashed against the Followers of Stroh.

"My judgedroids will handle this Conqueror's army. We shall deal with him and Celd now."

"How about we take them into another dimension." Fortune said.

"What are you implying?" Judge asked.

"I'm saying instead of facing them in your city and destroying your property. Much less the world, let's take them into another dimension and face them there. That way there's no escape for them."

Judge stared.

"Open the way, Enchanter."

Fortune moved his hands and twirled his fingers. Only the index and ring fingers were raised as the portal opened. Through the flash of the portal, Celd and Stroh appeared in the throne room.

"Where are you going?" Celd grinned.

"We need to move now!" Fortune said.

From the portal came a bright flash of light, knocking everyone back. Through the light appeared the Mystic Father. Fortune's eyes saw him and he immediately fell to his knees. Celd looked up and saw him. Stroh was unsure who he was. Huang and Tom also fell on their feet with Morhana following. Judge remained standing. His eyes showed the disgust he had for the Mystic Father.

"You're here?!" Celd said.

"I am. Because I cannot allow one of your kind to continue roaming this world."

"I do not know who you are." Stroh said, raising his hands to blast the Mystic Father.

"I will not be harmed this day."

The Mystic Father moved his arms as he pulled Fortune, Huang, Tom, Morhana, and Judge into the portal and closed it before Celd and Stroh could make an attack. Through the portal, the group found themselves in another dimension. A dimension shrouded in dark vioely colors and moving lights which resembled the Northern Lights.

"Where are we?" Judge asked.

"You're in the Mystic Dimension." The Mystic Father answered. "A place of my own dwelling."

"Why bring us here?" Fortune asked.

"Because I must tell all of you who's truly behind everything that has happened. It is not Celd nor Stroh. The being behind the attacks on the Citadel as well as the strange darkness in the air is a sorcerer known as Spellface."

"I've never heard of this Spellface." Fortune said.

"I warn you because he knows you're here and he is coming. Now, prepare yourselves for his arrival and do what you must to defeat him."

"Where will you be?" Judge asked.

"I will be where I always am. Close to my apprentices."

The Mystic Father vanished through the dimension's light as the group looked around at the dimension.

"We must get ready." Morhana said. "This Spellface is coming. I can feel his essence drawing near."

IV

YOU WISHED TO SEE ME?

"How can you feel his presence?" Huang asked.

"I just can. It's an eerie feeling. I know he's coming and he knows we're here."

"Then we must prepare ourselves." Fortune said.

"Mentor, what must we do once he arrives?" Tom asked.

"We fight. It is our only option."

Fortune turned and saw Judge watching something on his forearm. He approached him and saw a screen playing. The footage was of Palace Judge with the judgedroids taking the fight to Stroh's followers. Fortune made a gesture of noise as Judge closed the screen and faced him.

"I see your droids are winning the battle."

"Judge's droids always win their battles. There is no losing matter in them."

Thunder cracked through the dimensional heavens, gathering their attention in full. From above a light beamed through the ceiling and from it hovered down a figure. Dressed in a blood-red tunic and cloak. The figure's mouth hidden by a covering. A lean body, yet fueled with mystical energy. Fortune saw as the figure descended in front of them. His eyes closed and once his feet touched the dimensional ground, the eyes opened. Staring a hole through the team.

"Who are you?" Tom asked.

"It's him." Morhana said. "The one the Mystic Father warned us about."

"This is Spellface." Fortune said.

"Spellface?" The figure said. "I haven't heard such a name in eons. I am proud it still carries the same weight of fear as ages past."

"No one fears you." Judge said. "Tell us why you've come and why you're doing what you're doing."

"Very well. The powers you sensed above in the material world comes from me. I am preparing for my return upon the earth and the energy needed to be just right."

"Going to Earth for what purpose?" Fortune questioned.

"To bring forth my rule. I have servants that need to be found. Two of them I have already spoken with."

Fortune sighed bitterly.

"Celd and this King Stroh."

"Indeed. That reminds me."

Spellface raised his eyes toward the heavens and stretched forth his arms. Above them a portal opened and Celd and Stroh entered the dimension, standing on both sides of Spellface.

"You brought them here!" Fortune said.

"They're with me. I need them if I shall defeat you all."

"You believe you can defeat Judge?"

"I can defeat anyone I truly desire. Now, how shall we do this?"

"We can do this simply." Fortune said. "Best you surrender now unless you want a fight."

"Fights are always a welcoming cause for change."

Spellface glared toward the five in front of him. His eyes glinted like a flash of light. He raised his right hand toward them and gave off a small hint of a laugh.

"You believe we'll face you outnumbered? Scandalous."

From Spellface's forehead appeared a third eye. The eye flashed a light toward the group, blinding them from seeing what's ahead. Spellface opened a portal and snatched both Huang and Morhana. Tossing them into the portal and closing it shut. The third eye disappeared as did the flashing of light. Fortune managed to regain his sight and noticed Huang and Morhana were not among them.

"Don't concern yourself. They're well."

"Where did you send them?"

"Earth. At your Citadel of all places."

"Why?"

"Because this fight needs to be an even line. Three against three. Meanwhile, your two allies will be busy with a fight of their own."

Back on Earth at the Citadel, Huang and Morhana arose from the ground as they found themselves back on Earth. Huang turned around and saw the Citadel.

"We're back."

"No." Morhana said. "We need to get back to them."

"Indeed. But, how? We have no means to open a portal back to the dimension. The Mystic Father did it for us."

"Then contact him to do it again."

"I'm sorry, Morhana. But that's not how it works. He comes to us when he so chooses. Not us to contact him for a visitation of need."

Morhana screamed as she let off a blast of energy into the wilderness. After the blast escaped their sight, the sound of a gruesome roar emitted from the tree line. Huang and Morhana heard it and stared at the wilderness.

"What did you hit?" Huang asked.

"I'm not sure. A bear perhaps."

"That was no bear."

The ground trembled as Huang and Morhana backed up toward the citadel as they could sense the dark energy coming from the wilderness. Through the trees, appeared an army of motionless beings. Dark, cold, and wicked. The beings gave off no sound. No expression.

"What are they?" Morhana asked.

"I recognize them clearly." Huang answered. "They're called the Moronic Ones."

"Moronic Ones? How come?"

"They're motionless beings from the darker dimensions. They serve masters of great sinister power. I believe they're being used by this Spellface being and he sent them here to kill us."

"They won't kill us." Morhana scoffed. "We're too skilled for them."

"You're correct on that one, my lady."

V

SORCERERS AND GODS

Spellface, Celd, and Stroh stood side-by-side facing Fortune, Tom, and Judge. Spellface raised his arms as the dimensional energy came down from above and circled his hands like a whirlwind. Celd strengthened himself to the point of his inward energy appearing on the outside surrounding his body like a living flame. Stroh stood still. No emotion. Nothing.
"What's the plan here?" Tom asked.
"I'll take Spellface." Fortune answered. "Judge, what about you?"
"Leave the Conqueror to me. Judge shall see if he is as powerful as he claims."
"Thomas, that leaves you with Celd. Are you sure you're prepared for him?"
"You taught me enough. I can take him."
Fortune nodded as the three faced off against the others.
"Shall we begin?" Spellface laughed.
Celd rushed into the air like a living bolt, Tom followed him. Stroh moved to the side of the grounds and Judge stepped to his own movements. Fortune and Spellface did not moved as they stared one another down. Around them, Celd clashed with Tom

in a battle of magical wits. Judge and Stroh faced each other down. A Conqueror against a dictator. Their battle was a mental one.

"I will not allow you to win this war, Enchanter." Spellface said.

"No need to worry about my victory. Let it be done."

Meanwhile back on Earth, Huang and Morhana are taking the battle to the Moronic Ones in the ruins of the Citadel. Clashing their own magical skills against the darker powers. Huang moved through them with a spear made of pure energy. The swipes and slashes shattered much of the Moronic Ones. Morhana fought against them as she summoned magical daggers, tossing them into the heads of the Moronic Ones.

"I told you we could take them." Morhana chuckled.

"Keep fighting until they're all dead." Huang answered. "Celebrate afterwards."

Morhana grinned as she enjoyed slaying the Moronic Ones.

Back in the Mystic Dimension, Fortune and Spellface are having a battle of magical energies. Fortune dodged the wind attacks of Spellface and conjured a whirlwind of his own. Made from the mystical energies of his own power. The whirlwind of mystics broke down Spellface's own to his amusement. Fortune conjured a shield of energy and a sword.

"Close combat? Is that what you want?"

"Only one way to find out."

Spellface conjured a blade of his own and the two clashed in combat. Moving with such speed, Spellface could keep up with Fortune's own mystical speed. Above them, Celd fired several blasts of energy toward Tom, only for him to snatch them in the air, returning them toward Celd. Impacting him with a great rush. Beneath them, Judge and Stroh stared down. No movement. Motionless in both mind and body.

"Are you truly a conqueror?" Judge asked.

"I am. I've conquered many worlds."

"Then, how come you're here aligning with sorcerers and gods?"

"I have my reasons."

"Your reasons have brought you before Judge and Judge will not allow you to continue your regular duties for I am the only conqueror in this world and in all the worlds that exist. There is no one else better than Judge."

"You're wrong." Stroh said. "There is one better than you and it is I."

"Enough of your words. Judge shall finish you off quick and steady."

Stroh rushed himself back as he fired energy blasts toward Judge. Judge did not move as he only raised his right hand, deflecting the energy as a shield formed around his body. Judge stared into Stroh's eyes.

"You do not realize who you're dealing with." Judge said. "I am not like those you've conquered. This day, you will be the one conquered."

Judge took the energy and turned it against Stroh, blasting him in the chest as he fell to the ground. Judge looked down at Stroh before gazing toward Fortune's battle with Spellface and Celd's fight with Tom above him. Judge nodded as he caught Stroh moving.

"Best you do not make anymore movements, Conqueror."

Spellface saw Stroh on the ground and Celd's energy being turned against him by Tom. He grunted and yelled for Celd's help. Celd looked down and landed in between Fortune and Spellface, attacking the Enchanter with more energy beams. Tom landed on the ground only to be knocked down by Spellface's whirlwinds. Judge saw them being attacked and only watched as he kept his eyes on Stroh.

"It appears the two of us combined are capable of defeating them." Spellface said.

"You are correct." Celd said.

Thunder cracked above them. An unusual sound in the Mystic Dimension. Spellface gazed upward as he saw a crack in the sky. The crack increased and burst open like a major explosion, blowing back everyone aside from Judge and Stroh across the dimension. Through the shroud of the explosion appeared a figure. Cloaked in midnight blue. Golden eyes and a rough appearance.

"Who is that?!" Spellface said.

Fortune looked and saw the figure land in between him, Tom, and Spellface. The figure faced Spellface and looked over toward Celd.

"It appears you're the cause of the darkness on Earth. I must stop you."

"Who are you?" Spellface asked.

"I am Creed. The Unholy Knight."

VI

A MYSTIQUE SORCERER

Fortune and Tom arose from the ground and stood next to Creed. Spellface could sense Creed's power and began to step back. Celd however stepped forward. His eyes were locked on Creed.

"How did you know what was happening here?" Fortune asked.

"I was informed by an ally of mine. They sent me here."

"Well, we appreciate your assistance in this."

"Celd, what are you doing?" Spellface asked.

"I want a shot at this Unholy Knight."

"I am not an easy adversary to deal with."

Celd scoffed at Creed's words.

"Bring forth your power."

Spellface leaped into the air with Fortune and Tom chasing him. Celd extended his hands, releasing energy blasts toward Creed. Creed dodged the attacks as his cloaked cape absorbed the energy. Creed turned to face Celd and released his own energy back at him. Meanwhile, Stroh arose from the ground as Judge watched him regain his balance.

"Are you capable of continuing this battle?" Judge asked.

"I am not someone who gives up easily."

"Judge can tell by your words."

Stroh turned to his left and saw Celd battling Creed and with a gaze to the sky, he saw Spellface being double-teamed in magic attacks by Fortune and Tom. Stroh faced Judge and grinned.

"My time here is done. We shall meet again, Sinister Judge."

"You will not leave here so easily."

The ground around Stroh glowed an emerald shine as Stroh vanished from Judge's sight. Judge sighed as he watched the ongoing battles in front of him. Crossing his arms and standing with ease. He saw Creed claw Celd in the chest as small droplets of blood fell to the dimensional floor. Judge saw something within Creed. A power he was not familiar with. It intrigued him.

"I shall learn of his power soon." Judge stated.

. In the air, Spellface continued firing mystical blasts as they're deflected by Fortune's shields.

"Tom, take the shot!"

Tom stretched his right hand and from his fingers fired lightning. The lightning struck Spellface in the chest, knocking the magical entity to the ground in front of Judge.

"Hmm." Judge said.

Fortune and Tom descended next to him as they glanced down at Spellface. Fortune knelt closer and recognized Spellface was unconscious. He looked up toward Tom and nodded.

"You did well." Fortune said.

"Thank you, mentor."

Tom's hands began to glow a dark blue as lightning consumed his hands, reaching his forearms, then shoulders, then his head. The lightning had covered his entire body. Yet, Tom was not harmed and Fortune could tell. Judge stood still watching it take place. The lighting sparked and evaporated like mist and Tom's appearance had changed. He appeared to look slightly older than before and Fortune smiled.

"It has come to pass. You are indeed a true sorcerer now."

"What do you mean?"

"He means your powers have revealed themselves to you. Your magic is different than the Enchanter. You have something beyond the others."

"Judge is right. You're no longer a student in the mystic arts. You are your own sorcerer now."

The loud bang of an explosion interrupted their conversation as they turned to see the origin of the sound only to find Celd on the ground with Creed standing over him. Creed glanced up to see Fortune, Tom, and Judge. He gave them a nod as he flew up into the air as the portal opened, giving him way of exit.

"What now?" Tom asked.

"I will take Spellface and Celd to a prison far from humankind. You return to the Citadel and make sure Huang and Morhana are well."

"Will do."

Tom opened a portal of his own and exited the Mystic Dimension. Fortune looked around and turned toward Judge.

"Where's Stroh?"

"He fled." Judge said. "Refused to continue our battle."

"He'll be back."

"And Judge will be waiting."

"I take it you'll be returning to your palace?"

"Indeed. But do not take this short event as a means of us becoming allies. We both share opposite views on the world and in the realm of magic. I will become the ultimate sorcerer and if you stand in my way, I will destroy you."

"You already know me, Judge. I will always be there to stop those like yourself."

"We shall see."

Judge waved his hand as a rift in the dimension opened. Through the rift, Fortune could see Judge's palace as he stepped though with the rift closing like lightning afterwards. Fortune took Celd and Spellface and placed them in a mystical prison. A prison humanity does not know exists. Even other magic wielders aren't aware of such a prison.

Tom returned to the Citadel, seeing the outside and interior covered in the dead bodies of the Moronic Ones and Stroh's followers. Standing on the outside were Huang and Morhana. Side-by-side. They glanced over toward the forest, seeing Tom. Huang sighed with relief and Morhana was glad.
"Seems you two took care of yourselves."
"We can handle some demons and techno-drones." Huang laughed.
"You're right about that." Morhana said with a smile.

Sometime later, Fortune rebuilt the Citadel with his magic abilities as Tom appeared to have a uniform of his own. Similar to Fortune and Huang's, but with a hint of voodoo layered throughout. Fortune saw it and was impressed.
"I take it the people will call you Thomas the Sorcerer."
"I would rather they call me Doctor Mysticism."
"Doctor Mysticism?" Fortune said. "Hmm. Your decision. Not mine."
Fortune looked out toward the wilderness and through the trees, he could see cities. Fortune knew his purpose was to protect the innocent and after the recent event, Fortune was prepared to protect more than humanity. But, the mystical realms as well.

DOCTOR DARK: DIMENSIONS AND SEASONS

I

A VALENTINE UNFOLDED

February the 14th, the time and season for where Cupid, the god of Yen and erotic love roams the earth. His bow and arrow placed in his hands as he flies through the skies over the couples on the ground. Many are consumed by the day of Valentine's Day, spending their money on things they assume will present pleasure toward their spouses. Cupid stays still in the sky, looking down at the couples. He laughs at them.

"If they only knew the truth of the matter."

Cupid flies down and begins firing his arrows to the people walking through the sidewalks. The arrows pierce them and immediately, they are consumed with the notion of making love right there on the sidewalks. Which they do without hesitation, they quickly remove their spouses' clothes as if they're on fire. The sounds of moans and groans echo through the small area of the town. Cupid hovered above the scene, with a big smile on his face.

"Drink your fill, humanity. Let your cup overflow with the love of your lives."

In the Astral Dimension, Darkous watches the event take place and is aware that gods such as Cupid should not be out in the public eye period. Beatrice stood by him as he prepared himself to travel down to earth and stop Cupid in his flight.

"How do you plan on stopping that boy?" Beatrice said. "I'm curious."

"Simple. Knock him down off his throne. When he hits the ground, he will know his time is finished."

Darkous flies out of the Astral Dimension, heading for earth.

Back on the earth, Carol Hunters and Malach HaMavet sit together at her apartment, researching the newly found evidence of folklore figures rising up across the world. From Cupid to Jack Frost to Father Christmas.

"None of this is making any logical sense." Carol said.

"Because logic and reason have nothing to do with what is taking place. We need to make sure these folklore figures dare not harm some innocent ones out there."

"Should you contact your Master?"

"He's preoccupied at the moment with what we're researching. He knew about these figures a while back and was prepping himself for when they came out of the shadows."

"So, when will he need our help?"

"Truthfully, he doesn't need our help. Besides, he will come to us when the circumstance applies for it."

"May I ask you a question?"

"What kind of question do you need to ask me, Carol?"

"You don't take part in their holidays do you?"

"I do not. The holidays belong to the world. As you should already know, I am in the world, but not of the world."

"I can see that."

"You should be the same. Don't take part in these events that the world throws in people's face. Its all for advertising and selling merchandise anyhow."

"Now, that I can believe."

Darkous flies through the dark skies of the earth as nightfall as set on Valentine's Day. In the clouds, sat Cupid and he could feel a presence coming closer to him. Cupid turned around and Darkous burst through the cloud, facing Cupid. Cupid rose up and aimed his arrow toward Darkous. The arrow didn't faze Darkous at any rate.

"I will shoot you!"

"Take the shot, boy." Darkous said. "I am standing right in front of you."

Cupid fires the arrow, but Darkous catches it in midair, breaking the arrow in half in his hand. Cupid pulled out two arrows and aimed them toward Darkous' chest.

"Take the shots." Darkous said. "Do it."

Cupid fired the two arrows, Darkous grabbed them and snapped them as well. Cupid continued to fire more arrows at Darkous, who destroyed them with his hands and a mist of darkness that appeared to consume them and turn them into dust.

"This is not a battle you should be fighting, boy." Darkous said. "Why are you out here beneath the First Heaven?"

"This is the time of the year where I'm meant to roam the earth. You've seen these humans. They turned a warm heart on this day. This day is my time to rule and my time to bless humanity. The love that I give is powerful enough to make humans do and say things they wouldn't ordinarily say or do."

"Do you ever take the time to listen to the words that proceed from your mouth?"

"I speak a certain way, Darkous. A way that is vastly different from any other god or entity."

"Unlike my Astral sister who seems to tolerate your actions, I will not do the same. You're going back to your domain, Cupid."

"No. I am not going back to my home just yet. I still have arrows to fire and more love to hand out. The day isn't over. My day isn't over. My time has not yet been completed!"

Darkous rushed and grabbed Cupid by his throat. Darkous took his bow and arrow, consuming them with darkness, leaving them as dust which fell to the ground. Cupid began to pout as he trued to reach down for the dust on the ground.

"How could you!"

"You're going back to your domain, Cupid. You're not meant to roam the earth with such freedom."

Darkous teleported away out of the clouds with Cupid still in his grasp. He returned Cupid to his domain, a dimension where the Greek gods resided. Somewhat of a Mount Olympus dimension. Cupid cried during his way in as Darkous left the dimension quick as lightning. Upon returning to the Astral Dimension, Darkous is greeted by Yen, another one of the Astrals and sister to him. She giggled at Darkous pushing back her long black hair. He knew why she was there and why she was laughing.

"You don't have to tell me." Yen said. "How did he react to seeing you?"

"The same as the others, sister." Darkous said. "Why are you here on such a short notice?"

"I felt the presence of Cupid roaming the earth and everyone knew how much I love to tolerate the young guy. Figured as much, it would be you to stop him and send him back on home."

"He does not need to be roaming the earth with such freedom."

"And you should?"

"This is not a test of favorites, Yen. What he committed on the earth to humanity will leave a troublesome taste in the mouths of many."

"I'm sure with Cupid's talents, humanity had a fine taste of something they're familiar with."

"Your toleration of him is the reason why I have to stop him."

"Since you stopped him, you are aware of the other folklores roaming the earth?"

"They're around. The key is they will not resurface until the appointed season and time. I am well aware of the seasons in which they will come out of the shadows and make themselves known and I will be ready for them."

"I'm sure you will, brother."

Yen walked toward the exit of the Astral Dimension. She turned back to Darkous and he looked at her. A word was not spoken form his mouth, just a stare. Yen shook her head and smiled at him.

"I will come back when I need to."

"Do what you must, sister."

"I will."

Yen left the Astral Dimension with only Darkous remaining as he sat in a chair and patiently waited for the arrival of another folklore figure to appear on the earth.

II

AN ISHTAR EVENING

In the time of ancient Mesopotamia, Darkous made his arrival and witnessed how the civilization was growing amongst them. Wearing a black and violet uniform with a black and violet cloak, Darkous visited the Assyrian cities of Nineveh, Asshur, and Arbela. The locations within northern Mesopotamia whom worshipped the goddess Ishtar, the counterpart to the Sumerian goddess Inanna and the Northwest Aramean goddess, Astarte. Darkous had spotted the Mesopotamians bowing down to her altars and worshipping her.

"For this cause, has destruction been brewing against them." Darkous said. "Their destruction is now at hand."

Darkous flew down toward the worshipping ceremony and crashed the altars with a swift blow. The Mesopotamians looked around in fear of what happened to their altar. They cried in pain and sadness, some were filled with anger and revenge. Crying out to Ishtar to reveal who had decimated their altars to her. In the midst of the coming night, Darkous landed on the soil, facing the angry Mesopotamians.

"I am the one who made your altars desolate." Darkous said. "I am the one who will show you what true power is."

The Mesopotamians roared at Darkous, yelling at him to be a false god and not a real deity like Ishtar. Darkous pitied the Mesopotamians for their idol worship. He raised up his hand and from the sky came down a dark cloud, covered in great darkness, which grabbed the angry Mesopotamians and swallowed them up. The scene frightened the other Mesopotamians nearby, who began to run away from the location. Screaming for Ishtar to assist them in ridding the land of Darkous.

"If your goddess is here, watching over you all, why hasn't she revealed herself to me?" Darkous said. "Besides, I already know where she is and I am only here to see her myself."

From the ground, erupted a mist and through the mist walked out Ishtar, who stood boldly in the face of Darkous, A woman with a beautiful appearance as he long hair sat still against her breasts, two wings of a bird on her back and her feet were those of an owls with three talons on each foot. She stood completely nude, carrying with her two crosses and by her feet stood two owls and two lions.

"I see that you've accepted my call, daughter of Anu." Darkous said. "You know why I am here."

"I am aware of your purpose in my territory, Astral One." Ishtar said. "I only presented myself to you for only one reason."

"What would be that reason, false idol?"

"To have the chance at killing an Astral entity and leaving its body for my worship to receive over and do with as they please."

"You are sick as sick as your worshippers. Taking part in sacred prostitutions and making these humans believe you have much power as He does."

"I have power and it has been proven with the help of the Mesopotamians."

"It is a shame that Tammuz and Gilgamesh aren't here to help you."

"They will be just fine. The only one who will have to worry about anything at this moment is you."

Ishtar raised up her hand and from the ground bolted out a smoke, which blinded Darkous. She screamed, unleashing the two lions and two owls to attack Darkous. The lions take a hold of his leg and arm, while the owls deal with his head. Darkous swings his arms against the owls, but their talons are strong and are holding his curly hair tightly. Ishtar stood quietly, only showing a faint smile on her face as she wipes her hair from her face.

"You're doing good over there, Darkous. A shame to see such a powerful figure die by my hand in such an easy fashion."

Darkous stared at Ishtar with his eyes glowing a dark blue. A shroud of darkness began to conjure up around his body and his legs. The lions released their holds against Darkous, running back to Ishtar. Darkous raised up the shroud, which grabbed a hold of both the owls, tossing them back at Ishtar.

"You do not know who you are dealing with, Pagan goddess!"

"I think I know who I'm dealing with."

"No, you don't."

Darkous turned his hand toward Ishtar, as the shroud of darkness swarmed toward her and immediately pulled her into its thick darkness, within the shroud, Ishtar couldn't see a thing, but only here the sound of a large whirlwind within the darkness. The wind blew heavily and the ground shook beneath her feet. The ground started to crack open and from the ground, Ishtar could see darkness and fire.

"What is such a place where fire domains?!" Ishtar said.

"It is a place where the wicked will enter once their time is done in this life. But, you, Ishtar, Pagan goddess, will not be sent there just yet. For I have a greater punishment for your ways on the earth."

"Such as what?"

"This."

Darkous raised up both his arms and from behind Ishtar

appeared a large block of stone. Though, the stone wasn't hard, but liquid. Darkous moved the stone wall toward Ishtar, which began to suck in her, the owls, and the lions. She screamed for mercy as the wall pulled her in and Darkous did not speak a word during her screams. The wall had taken her and once Darkous released his hold on the stone wall, it became as solid as the ground, trapping Ishtar, the owls, and the lions within it. Darkous later placed the stone wall within one of the building structures within Mesopotamia.

"Until the appointed time comes, you will be entrapped within this stone wall, Ishtar."

Darkous walked away and from the sky came down Gabriel the Archangel. He stated he needed to tell Darkous of the future and what will come of Ishtar.

"In the distant future, the world will partake in a yearly event where they will paint eggs and present the rabbit as the idol. They will also make a worship toward a false leader, one who is a mockery of the coming leader."

"You tell me this because of what purpose?"

"You will be there to see it unfold and you will be there to witness its end."

"Will I?"

"Not only for the event, but there will be other mighty ones that will make themselves known throughout the earth, where humanity will celebrate their days of birth and their days of reveling. I warn you this day so you can be ready when the appointed times come."

"I understand you meaning for telling me this, archangel."

Gabriel flew off into the sky as Darkous walked through the lands of the altars to Ishtar. On the ground, Darkous had found a setting where there had been laid eggs, covered in blood, laying on the graves. Darkous nodded.

"Ah." Darkous said as he stomped the blood-covered eggs

before leaving Mesopotamia.

III

ALL HELL OWES

All Hallows' Eve, the event of the Celtics and those who celebrate the dead. The modern-day term used across many countries is Halloween. Many of the children in a small county get together and begin going to house to house, trick or treating for candy. The clear night sky is suddenly covered with dark clouds, forming over the county, the children look upward as do their parents as they witness both Darkous and Beatrice coming down from the clouds and landing on the roadway in the middle of a section of homes.

"So, he's going to be right in this spot?" Beatrice said.

"This exact spot." Darkous said. "He'll show himself when he wants to be seen by us. Remember, he is a clever sneaky one."

"Aren't most of them from time to time."

They stand in the middle of the road, waiting for someone to appear to them. Nearby one of the homes, a young boy approaches Darkous and Beatrice. She looked down at the boy and stared. Showing a smirk toward him as the young boy tapped Darkous on his arm.

"The young lad wishes a word with you, Darkous." Beatrice said. "Maybe he will have an answer concerning our business here."

"Let's wait and see."

"Excuse me, sir." The young boy said. "I'm sorry to disturb you, but."

"What do you want of me, young one?"

"That man over there said he wants to speak to you."

"What man?"

"The man with the glowing pumpkin for a head."

"Is that right?"

Darkous turned around quickly and found himself and Beatrice staring at the Jack O' Lantern. Somewhat nonrelated to Mr. Pumpkinhead. Though, both possess a pumpkin for a head, yet Jack O' Lantern's head glows as of a fire kindling within it.

"You have been looking for me, Astrals?" Jack O' Lantern said with a graveling voice.

"We have and we knew you would rise out of the darkness on this particular day and season." Darkous said.

"This day belongs to me. While the little ones search out for treats to consume, I search out those of the fearful. Their ways of being terrified give me my strength and my power."

"Like you need anymore power than you already possess." Beatrice said. "Now, you have two options standing in front of you. You can either turn yourself over and return to your own dimension and leave this world or you can make the attempt in keeping yourself here until the day is done and get yourself destroyed by me and Darkous. So, what is your answer, glowing ball?"

Jack O' Lantern grunted with his glowing smile facing Beatrice.

"Two choices. That's all you have to offer me on this day? My day?"

"Choose one." Darkous said. "Make it a quick decision for your own self."

"My answer is option number two."

Jack O' Lantern raised up his hand, projecting flames from it and throwing it toward Darkous and Beatrice. The flames appeared as a ball and knocked both pf them into one of the nearby homes. Darkous and Beatrice stand up atop the debris of the home's wall and front door with Jack O' Lantern standing there, facing them with both his hands consumed with fire.

"Come on, Astrals. Do what you must to complete your mission."

"We will do so, pagan one." Darkous said. "Feel the true powers of an Astral entity."

Darkous raised up his hands as the wind began to pick up. The children and parents around the area immediately ran into the homes they stood close by and locked the windows and doors while the wind increased in strength and speed. Darkous turned over to Beatrice and nodded his head.

"Do what you can."

"I will."

Beatrice turned her hands around in form of twirls and waves. From her hand appeared a glowing green energy, which she projected and shot at Jack O' Lantern. Hitting him in his chest, he stumbled for a second in time, regaining the strength in his legs.

"What kind of power was that?" Lantern said. "It made me lose my stance for a moment."

"Call it my power." Beatrice said. "Us Astrals might be similar to a degree, but we were all created with an individual purposes and gifts of power."

Beatrice waved her hands again and pulled them both apart from each other, creating a wave that dove through the abdomen of Lantern. Grunting in pain as he held his ribs. The fire in his head beginning to dim as he is becoming weaker. Beatrice continued to release energy waves toward Lantern while Darkous increased the power of the wind and from the sky came down a cloud of great darkness. A thick blanket of darkness.

"I have my gifts which make me what I am." Beatrice said. "While Darkous on the other hand...."

"I am the Keeper of the Cosmos." Darkous said. "I control the darkness the generations of Man gaze upon when the moon shines down and when the light is absent from their sight. That power was given to me to control and now, you will feel the wrath of such power."

The wind grabbed Lantern and carried him into the thick darkness. Lantern looked and found himself high in the air, looking down at Darkous and Beatrice. He roared at them with anger as his eyes began to glow with fire purging out of them.

"You think this can stop me?! You believe your little dominion prison can hold me?! I have power! This is not the end of my time nor my day!"

"Go back to your domain, pagan creature." Darkous said, pushing the darkness into the abyss, with Lantern trapped within its crosshairs. Roaring at them until silence consumes the county. The children and parents slowly walk outside of the homes, around Darkous and Beatrice.

"Young ones and old, listen to these words and take heed of them." Darkous said. "You partake in such a day that even you do not understand what is becoming of you. Mothers and fathers must learn the truth in all matters and teach them to their children. For if you do not do such a task, destruction will always be at your door and after the destruction comes death."

Darkous and Beatrice leave the small county in a pillar of darkness. Returning to the Astral Dimension. Within the dimension, Darkous spots another woman walking around the area. He approaches her as Beatrice goes to the other side of the area.

"Is is something to see you here, Beauty." Darkous said.

"I just had to come by and visit once more." Beauty said. "Its been a very long time."

"Where have you been since the last millennia?"

"Going around the earth and entering many dimensions. There is so much that takes place which the humans have no idea even exists. Sometimes, I feel sorry for them for the things they do not know. Things that could help them or destroy them."

"Things will be revealed to them when the time calls for it. Right now, they must prepare their hearts and themselves for the things to come."

"I know. I see you've been busy over the past few months in earth time. Dealing with the other mighty ones that have risen from their dwelling places."

"They must know their place and role in His creation. Nothing more than that should they do."

"So, what is next on your agenda, Darkous?"

"To await the world's day of Thanksgiving. I know for sure there will be several mighty ones who will make themselves known to the world and they are a fierce some deities."

IV

THEY GIVE A THANKFUL MASSACRE

The day of thanks they've said over centuries past and present. The day is celebrated and partaken by many that live within the culture of the western world. The day is known as Thanksgiving Day and most of the world, particularly in the west. Meanwhile, in the lands of Scandinavia, the Norse gods have arisen and are coming towards the western world to cause chaos.

In the Astral Dimension, Darkous sat and watched as the Norse gods made their way toward the west. Uncertain of their goals and their actions, Darkous prepared himself for the journey to confront them head on. Darkous left the Astral Dimension, going down to the earth. Taking place on the earth, Carol and Malach are continuing their search for the Mythologists' secret base.

The Norse gods, ranging from Loki to Woden had begun to make their way into the western lands, overlooking the people on their Thanksgiving Day. Loki laughed as he watched them sitting at the tables and eating.

"Look at those mortals. They're stuffing their faces as if this is their last day to feast!"

"A custom not too different from the souls of Valhalla." Loki declared to himself "It is not different at all."

While moving through the air, the wind bolted against them with a strong current. Loki looked around the sky to discover the wind's source. He didn't bother to scout any longer as he only enjoyed the possible interference.

"Maybe Thor decided to come along." Loki said.

"Do not underestimate him. The only reason I'm here is because I was allowed to come."

In the air, the clouds darkened and from them emerged Darkous, catching the attention of Loki. They only stared at him, seeing him in awe and as an intruder to their plan. Loki pointed toward Darkous as if he was some strange god that came from the realm of Hel.

"Did Hel send a soldier of hers to stop me?"

"I am not one of Hel's mischievous one." Darkous said. "I am Darkous of the Astrals and I am here to cease your plans of invasion."

"Why don't you go along and take your business elsewhere, Astral. Leave me be, so I can do what I've come to do."

"I will not leave you to your own devices. Return to the lands of Scandinavia and return to your realm of existence."

"I will once I finish my work." Loki said with a smile.

"Then you leave me with no other choice."

Darkous created a energy ball of shadows and slammed it into Loki, causing him to roll through the air. Loki took the attack and stopped himself from billowing in the air. He stared at Darkous and laughed.

"You want a fight do you!"

"A fight will not happen this day. Return to your own land and leave these humans be."

"You can't do this! Woden insisted on us making a great work this day."

"That won't be necessary." Darkous said coldly.

Elsewhere, Carol Hunters and Malach HaMavet have found the location of the Mythologists. Their home it seemed. Carol attempted to pick the lock on the door, yet Malach had other intentions as he drew his sword and shoved it in between the door and the wall. Jerking the blade, the door opened with only a crack. Entering the home, they quickly see dozens of artifacts and books. Malach recognized one of the artifacts on the wall.

"That sword. People have been searching for it for many decades."

"And it's just here." Carol said. "In their home."

"We can't take it with us. They'll know we were here."

"Ok. What's the plan now?" Carol wondered.

"We leave. This is their place of residence. We know it now and that's all we came to learn."

Continuing, Darkous and Loki speak about Woden's plans for the people during their Thanksgiving. Darkous continued to refuse Loki's warnings and simply asked for Woden to make himself known. After those words left the lips of Darkous, thunder roared in the heavens and Woden made himself known. Standing on the ground like a homeless man. A staff in his right hand, two ravens on his shoulders, and his long brim hat that shrouded his eye. Darkous approached him and stared.

"Why are you here, Norse god?"

"Who are you meant to be? One of the darker ones lurking around this world?"

"I am the Keeper of the Cosmos and you will answer the questions I speak toward you."

Woden scoffed.

"What questions do you have for me?"

"Why have you come to the United States during their Thanksgiving? For what purpose does it serve you and your kind?"

"We came to see how they operate on certain days. We seek no harm upon them. Only a means to study and observe."

"That's not what Loki had mentioned to me."

"Don't mind him. He's going through his own matters this day. That is why he came along."

Darkois stared at the two Norse gods. His eyes slowly turning a dark blue.

"You both cannot remain here any longer. Return to your own land and remain there as you were created to do."

"We're not going anywhere!" Loki screamed.

"Yet we are." Woden said.

"What?! What are you saying?!"

"We came here to observe these humans during their holy day. We saw all we needed to see. Now, let us return to our land."

"I will not leave this place until I can do what I Yen."

"Enough." Darkous said. "I shall send you back to Scandinavia where you belong."

Darkous raised his right hand as the darkness consumed Loki from below, dragging him down as if he was entering the depths of Sheol. Loki starched to remain above ground, but the darkness was too powerful. Even for a Norse god. With one last scream, Loki was gone as was the darkness. Woden turned toward Darkous and showed a sign of respect toward the Keeper of the Cosmos' power.

"We will meet again, Astral." Woden said, as he transformed into a raven and flew away.

"I will be waiting." Darkous replied silently.

V

CHRISTMAS TO REMEMBER IN A SEASON

A city covered by snowfall. A season familiar to many. Yet, in this city, a vile nature loomed over the residents as they all came from their homes to celebrate their holiday. A time where heathenism arose greatly. This holiday is known among them as Saturnalia. The Winter Solstice had come and the residents took part in its coming in the same manner as Saturnalia.

Above them in the air was Darkous. Watching them from above with disgust on his face. He knew their kind and often clashed with them and their gods. This night was no different than the others as Darkous landed on the ground in the midst of the celebrations. The residents paused and stared at the dark-clad figure. Darkous' unseen pupils measured each of the humans as they looked at him with disfigured expressions.

"Who are you supposed to be?" One of the residents said.

"I am Darkous of the Astrals and I have come to end your wicked celebrations."

"Wicked?!" said another resident. "Who are you to call us wicked?"

"Your actions speak for themselves. I have come to make sure you do not repeat them again on this earth."

"Run on home, you fool!" A third resident yelled.

"I will be home." Darkous said. "Once my task is complete."

"And what is your task exactly?"

"Cleansing this place of you all."

Darkous extended his arms as the misty shadows conjured themselves from the pavement and the dirt of the ground. The darkness consumed the residents with ease as they did their best to fight back. The shadows were too thick and too thin for the resident to retaliate with punches and kicks. It was like fighting the air in their manner. Once the residents were gone, Darkous turned around and saw a figure standing in the empty street. Their eyes locked and the Keeper of the Cosmos knew who the figure was.

"I knew you would make yourself known." Darkous said.

"This is my season. My time."

"As they'll always say. Father Christmas."

"You've taken my servants. Where will I now find those who will worship me to the greatest extent of their abilities?"

"Is not my sister, Materialisa not enough or are the souls of humanity worth more the damage you cause?"

"Materialisa does what she wants. I do what I was created to do. Humans were designed to be my servants. It is nature."

"You shall have none. Worship does not belong to you. Nor to me."

Father Christmas pointed into the air as a slew of reindeer arrived. Rushing to ambush Darkous. With one snap from his fingers, Darkous summoned a portal of darkness which took the reindeers by storm. They were no more.

"What have you done to my deer?"

"Sent them to a place where they'll no longer be required. It is time for you to leave, Father Christmas. Now."

Anger kindled within Father Christmas like a boiling pot of oil. He went to approach Darkous as the Keeper of the Cosmos stretched forth his hand as a shade of darkness formed through his palm. Father Christmas stopped and only glared.

"Leave this world." Darkous said. "Return to the duties you were created for."

Father Christmas sighed with bitter in his voice. He went away, pointing toward Darkous with a proclamation that it would not be their final meeting. Darkous agreed as Father Christmas took off with a swift wave of snow. Darkous turned around and looked out toward the empty streets. The iniquity which covered the streets prior to his arrival was gone. With a nod, Darkous took off into the night sky. Unseen in the darkness of the night.

VI

A NEW YEAR DAWNS AND TURNS

The Roman New Year was set to dawn as the world began to take part in their celebration of the moment. However, in the dimensions unseen by the natural eye, The Gate of Time was set to repeat its previous actions. Every year, the gate would open at the start of the new year and lead to a close on the final day of the previous year. The gate was prepared to be open by Janus himself. The Roman god of beginnings and ends. He stood by the gate in the dimension with its swirling clouds and moving mists of water. The entire dimension looked like a major storm was coming. A dark blue hue shrouded the dimension with shades of black and white intermixing through the clouds.

"The time is almost upon me." Janus said, standing at the doors of the gate. "A new year approaches and changes will occur."

"Yes." said a voice from behind Janus in the dark. "Change will come."

Through the darkness, Janus sought to know who was within thee dimension he was familiar with. From the shroud of the dark came forth Darkous. His eyes, glaring with a golden hue as he stared toward Janus.

"Keeper of the Cosmos." Janus said. "Why is it you have come here on this day?"

"To make a change. The world of humanity no longer needs your gate to bring forth new beginnings and ends. They have the power to do so themselves."

"Are you telling me to leave my post?"

"I am."

"Under who's authority do you speak from? Because Astrals do not have the authority to declare who or what must leave their duty."

"You are right on that matter. My orders come from a much higher source."

"What source do you speak of?"

"You know who I'm speaking of." Darkous declared. "Now, leave the gate and return to your true domain. Time will take care of itself."

Janus stepped back, refusing to leave as he drew forth a sword from his side. Pointing it toward Darkous.

"I do not want to use this!"

"No need." Darkous replied.

"Well then. Before we enter this scuffle of a time, I must give you a warning. A personal one."

"Personal warnings do not bring fear upon an Astral."

"Oh. I'm not seeking to bring forth fear. Only truth in a certain matter. Beware of the Dark Hunters. For they search for you, Darkous and in time they will find you and only then will your future be certainly clear."

Darkous stared as Janus grinned.

"Time to go." Darkous said.

The floor beneath Janus transformed from the sapphire marble to a pit of darkness. Janus screamed as he fell down the hole and Darkous sealed it with only a wave of his right hand. He looked up as the gate opened, revealing the New Year had come. With a nod, Darkous turned away from the gate and vanished through the mist of darkness.

Sometime later, in the Astral Dimension, Darkous was visited by Michael the Archangel. Expecting some details regarding an ongoing event in the earth, Michael had come to confirm the words spoken by Janus. The Dark Hunters are real and they're coming for the Keeper of the Cosmos.

"Let them come." Darkous said. "For I shall show them darkness in the beauty of the light."

HEAVEN HAS CALLED: MAGICKS AND MYSTICISM

I

THE HOVERING DARKNESS

Standing in the Revelation Center within the main office, Travis Vail spoke with Gabriel Abraham. The two familiars with the supernatural after their individual and team-up investigations. Vail arrived at the Center to speak to Abraham concerning the darkness which is looming over the earth. Evan Wyatt and Andrea Corraline, Abraham's apprentices entered the office, seeing Vail. Abraham informed Vail he was aware of the darkness and could not track down the source.

"I'm sure there are other ways in finding this darkness." Evan Wyatt said.

"I'm sure, lad." Vail replied. "I'm sure."

"So, tell me what you have planned?" Abraham asked.

"I suggest we get the group together."

"The group? Are you sure this is big enough to gather everyone once again?"

"I'm certain. We can't be the only ones aware of this darkness. The magic in the air that follows it gives off a stench. Smells just like-"

"Brimstone." Abraham said. "I know."

"The only question is where do we start."

"I have the answer." said a voice entering the Center.

Vail, Abraham, Evan, and Andrea stepped out from the office to greet the visitor and upon their turn of the hall, they saw Papa Afterlife. Vail smirked and shook his head while Abraham greeted Afterlife.

"He always shows up at a time like this." Vail smiled. "It's written."

"This is no joking matter, Travis Vail."

"I know. I'm just wondering what you have that pertains to this darkness we're trying to stop."

"I know the cause of it and who's responsible."

"You know this how?" Abraham asked.

"I have my sources and they tell me everything. Both good and evil."

"Who's responsible?" Vail questioned.

"A man named Mordecai Gascoyne. He's a powerful foe. Some say he's responsible for the creation of the Specter Errant. But, we're not certain of that matter. However, this darkness that looms over us all, his hand is upon it and he's not alone."

"Who else is with him?"

"Right now, we are not certain. It could be anyone of our adversaries from the past or newcomers seeking to make a name for themselves."

Vail cocked his head and turned toward Abraham.

"I think we need to get the group together."

"On that you are correct."

"Gather your allies." Afterlife said. "And do it quickly. Gascoyne grows with more power by the minute."

"I'll call Cindy." Vail said. "See what she's currently up to."

II

THE ATTACK OF MANCHESTER

The Man Called Fable took his daily stroll through the city of Manchester. Walking about as his eyes were open to anything unusual. Particularly anything of the magical sort. He was still amazed by the thought of the civilians' ignorance to the existence of magical beings in the midst of living in a world with the risen heroes and the past events which have happened throughout the world. During his stroll, Fable saw someone peculiar. He moved with a quicker pace to reach them and inching closer, the person vanished from his sight.

"The hell?"

Fable searched for the disappearing figure. Looking at every turn he made. Taking another turn, facing back to where he came, he stopped quickly as he saw Cinderella.

"Funny seeing you here." Fable smirked. "Doesn't London need its unseen hero?"

"Yes. However, during one of my recent investigations, I came into some information regarding magical beings. That's why I've come. I've heard a lot about magical beings sighted around this city."

"Such rumors are indeed true. Magical beings are here. It just takes one to find out where they dwell."

"Oh. And you won't mind helping me in doing so?"

"Wait what?"

"You deal with them all the time. According to your words of your work. Why don't you aid me in this case, help me solve it and we can go our separate ways."

Fable was unsure of what to say toward Cinderella. As he stood there conjuring up some reply, the sky above them bolted with a red streak of lightning mixed with blue and white strikes. Fable and Cinderella gazed up as the civilians began to run. The lightning formed a portal and through the portal came forth Emblem. Fable stepped forward and pointed. Similar to how a child sees an animal.

"Oh shit!" Fable said. "It's Emblem!"

"Who?" Cinderella asked.

"Holy shit! We've been searching for this guy for months. Nearly a year at this point! Oh man, Pandora's going to be thrilled."

Emblem hovered in the air, overlooking Manchester as he could hear the screams and cries of the scattered civilians. The honking of the vehicles. It savored him how the fear grew upon his presence.

"Ah! The human world. It has been sometime."

"Hey! Emblem!" Fable yelled. "Down here!"

"What are you doing?!" Cinderella said.

"Getting his attention. No worries."

Emblem glared down, seeing Fable and Cinderella. His eyes grew red at the sight of Fable.

"You." Emblem growled. "I remember you."

"You do? Really?"

"You and that peasant Pandora sought to take me out. Yet, it seems destiny has another option in my favor."

"Why come back anyway dude?"

"I have been summoned. Summoned for a great task. In which I shall have the pleasure of destroying you and this world."

Fable grinned and shook his head while Cinderella was prepared for the possible battle.

"Nah. Not happening." Fable said, pulling out his revolver and taking the shot.

The magical round pierced Emblem's armored chest. Not phasing the magical being. Emblem grinned at the attack and returned to the portal. Fable took more shots as the portal closed.

"Dammit!" Fable said.

"What now?"

"Right now, your case is gonna have to wait. Emblem's back and on Earth. This is not good."

Cinderella reached into her jacket pocket, taking out her phone and she read the ID.

"Looks like Emblem's not the only concern we're going to have."

Back at the Center, Vail sat in an office speaking with Cinderella on the phone while Abraham attempted to find a way to contact Creed and Death Chaser. He had no means in such a possibility. Their first encounter was only by chance to an extent. Afterlife approached Abraham, seeing how he was seeking to contact the other members.

"You have to remember." Afterlife said. "Most of the team are supernatural beings. They cannot be contacted by the means of phones. Such as Vail is with Cinderella."

"I'm aware, brother."

"Then, you should consider other means of contact. Where do they often dwell?"

"Various locations. Creed is often found atop churches or temples. Chaser comes and goes. Outlander and Manhunter do as they please. Shaw is in England, so I'm curtained Cinderella will contact him. That's how this is I guess."

"Fair point. Do what you can."

Vail stood at the door of the office, still speaking on the phone.

"First thing, I don't know who this Emblem bloke is supposed to be. Right now, we need you here with us. Things are about to get worse."

"Fable is with me right now." Cinderella said on the other line.

"Tell him to come along as well. Maybe this Emblem guy might be connected to this sudden darkness. Oh and another thing, Cindy."

"What's that?"

"Do us a favor and wake up Shaw, please."

"I'll see what I can do."

"Much appreciated." Vail hung up the phone.

From that moment, Vail returned to Abraham's office, seeing Afterlife standing at the front of the desk.

"What have you found?" Afterlife asked.

"Well, for starters, Cindy is coming here and she's bringing the Fable guy along. Apparently, Manchester was visited by some guy called Emblem. Came through a portal above the city in broad daylight."

"Emblem?" Abraham said.

"Yeah. Said he's some powerful magic bloke. Fable apparently knows him and Emblem knows him. There's a history there."

"I've heard of the name Emblem." Afterlife said.

"Oh, you have?" Vail said. "Well, tell us more."

"Emblem is a powerful figure in the Rift. The magical realm outside of this one. Through much growth in power, he was cast out by the Hidden Four to keep balance in the realm. Unfortunately, he found a way to return and in that, war was started. It was only in recent time that Emblem appeared on the earth. Last I heard, he was defeated by Fable and Pandora, an assistant to the Four."

"We met Pandora once." Vail said. "We've seen what she can do."

"Anyone else we may need to contact?" Abraham asked.

Vail thought and smirked.

"You have someone in mind, don't you?" Afterlife said.

"We need to visit the Doctor."

"What Doctor?" Afterlife questioned.

"He's speaking of the Supreme Enchanter."

"Ah." Afterlife answered. "The Doctor Fortune."

III

A VISIT TO THE ENCHANTER

Vail and Abraham arrived at the Citadel of Enchantment. Seeing the ruined grounds surrounding the magical structure intrigued Vail. He knelt down, touching the grass, seeing scorch marks in the dirt.

"What is it?" Abraham asked.

"Something happened here. Not long ago."

"Let's ask and see."

Approaching the doors, they took their steps and the doors opened. Allowing them inside. Vail knew Fortune was aware of their presence. The two entered the Citadel and within mere seconds a mystical blast of fire blew past them. They ducked the flames and saw Tom Bradley standing in the center.

"It's the apprentice." Vail said. "You look slightly different."

"I had a change."

"Travis Vail." said a voice coming from the staircase.

Vail and Abraham glanced up as they saw Doctor Fortune hovering in the air as he moved toward them. His feet touched the floor as he nodded to them in a greeting matter.

"Spirit-Seeker." Fortune said.

"Doc Fortune." Vail said. "Nice to see you again."

"I see you brought the Devilhunter as well."

"I wouldn't be here unless it was urgent."

"I understand. So, why have you both come?"

"First, I want to ask." Vail said, looking around the Citadel. "What happened here? I sense the spirit of heaviness in certain places."

"We recently went through a battle. Fought some new foes. Teamed with adversaries. Suchlike."

"Must've been a tough battle." Abraham said.

"It was. Now, tell me why you've come."

"The hovering darkness." Vail answered. "We've discovered the source and we need your help in this matter."

"The source? We've already taken out the source of the darkness."

"I'm afraid you're wrong." Abraham said.

"Then, who or what's the source of this darkness?"

"Some bloke called Mordecai Gascoyne. A sorcerer we've been told."

"Gascoyne." Fortune said. "The name is familiar. However, we've never come across anyone with it. What's your plan regarding all of this?"

"We've already sent out word to the others we can contact." Vail said. "We need the others we can't contact. Like Creed, Death Chaser, and so on."

"Creed I can contact. He aided us during our recent endeavor. I'll do what I can to contact the others.

"When is Cinderella arriving?" Abraham asked Vail.

"Traveling will take too long. She needs a portal."

"I can help with that." Fortune said.

Fortune stepped to the outside as the doors open on their own. A movement of the hands and a portal had opened. Waiting for several seconds and through the portal walked Cinderella, Fable, and the Ghost of England. Once they stepped foot on the soil, Fortune closed the portal.

"Wasn't expecting a quick arrival." Cinderella said. "Anyhow, thanks for the portal."

"No problem. What Vail and Abraham have told me, this situation is certainly an urgent one."

"Good to see you again, Doc." Fable said.

"Same here." Fortune slowly spoke.

"Now, we need to find the Unholy Knight and Chaser." Vail said. "I'm not sure how we can contact Outlander and Manhunter."

"They'll arrive when necessary." Fortune said. "It's what they do."

Vail nodded toward the Ghost of England.

"See you haven't missed a step." Vail said with a smile.

"How can I miss a step?"

"It's just an expression, Shaw." Abraham answered. "Not an actual question."

They returned inside the Citadel and began coming up with a plan to contact the others. Fortune suggested they head to Connecticut where Creed is often sighted. Abraham agreed. The Chaser roams the earth, finding him would be a difficult matter, yet Fortune believes he can communicate with the Soul of Retribution. As for Outlander and Manhunter, when the time is right, they will make themselves known. It is in their nature to appear when needed.

"Let's go find Creed." Fortune said. "Best we start there."

"I'm all for it." Vail replied.

"Not all of us need to travel to Connecticut." Abraham said. "I'll go with Fortune to find Creed. Best you guys do what you can to contact the Chaser."

"You're not wrong." Cinderella said.

Fortune and Abraham walked through a portal, arriving in Hartford past midnight. Abraham stepped forward, finding themselves in front of a Catholic Church. He looked up to the top and saw something flowing with the cool wind.

"I think I found him." Abraham said pointing upwards.

"It's him." Fortune said. "I'll go talk to him. Give him all the details he needs. You wait here."

Fortune hovered in the air toward the top. Reaching it, he saw the golden eyes of Creed through the darkness and nodded.

"Creed. It's me."

Creed glared toward Fortune and nodded back.

"Intriguing we meet again so soon."

"I know. I appreciate your assistance against Spellface and Celd back in the Mystic Dimension. We surely needed it."

"It was a call I could not refuse. Now, what brings you to my domain?"

"The darkness. Some of our allies have discovered the source. I thought it was Spellface. But I was wrong. The source of this darkness comes from a sorcerer called Mordecai Gascoyne. We're trying to get the team back together to find him and stop his work."

"You speak of the Spirit-Seeker and the Devilhunter?"

"I do. They're busy trying to find the Chaser."

"I can do that for you."

"You can? How?"

"The Chaser and I have a connection in the spiritual realm. We can communicate without speaking a word. Give me a moment."

Creed stood still as if he was frozen. His head looking up toward the heavens. His golden eyes focused. Within a moment of time, the Chaser appeared atop the church, holding the head of a creature in his right hand. Fortune stepped back to avoid the severed head.

"That was fast." Fortune said.

"Time moves different." Creed replied. "Chaser, good you arrived."

"What is happening?" The Chaser asked.

"The darkness. We found the source and we're going to stop it."

"Is it Demonicronto?"

"Afraid not."

"Good." The Chaser nodded. "That's good."

Creed moved from his post as they followed Fortune back to Abraham. Come own from the church, Abraham was startled by Creed and the Chaser's arrival. A leap from the top as Fortune levitated down.

"Devilhunter." Creed said.

"Creed."

"I know about your battle with the Coven." The Chaser said.

"You do?"

"I have something for you. But, it'll have to wait till after this darkness is destroyed."

"Understandable."

Fortune opened a portal and they returned to the Citadel. Vail and Cinderella looked out, seeing the portal opening as they walked through it. Vail nodded.

"That was quick." Cinderella said.

"Indeed."

The team greeted each other in their own ways as Fortune and Vail sought to figure out how they could communicate with Outlander and Manhunter. While thinking of ideas, Outlander appeared inside the Citadel, standing behind Fortune and Vail at the table.

"You sought me out."

Vail jumped as Fortune turned slowly to see Outlander. From the doors appeared Manhunter, who levitated toward them at the table. Fable watched as it was all ongoing and only nodded with a slight smirk.

"I guess this is how it is."

"Good of you guys to finally show up." Vail said. "We need your help."

"We know why you're all here, Travis Vail." Outlander said.

"We are aware of the darkness." Manhunter said. "We've known for quite some time."

"And you didn't tell us anything?" Abraham asked.

"It was not our time to speak of such events." Outlander stared. "You were not prepared during such a time. Yet, now, you stand to face it."

"This Mordecai Gascoyne," Fortune said toward Outlander. "You've seen him?"

"I have. He's a powerful man. Trained in the arts for a very long time."

"Training doesn't matter." Manhunter said. "He can be defeated the same as anyone else. You just need to find the weakness."

Cinderella walked forward, raising her hand as a joking gesture.

"It's good that we're all here, but we need to know where to start at finding Gascoyne."

"The wilderness." Outlander said.

"Wilderness." Vail said. "What wilderness are you talking about?"

"Any of them. The darkness looms over the earth. It will make itself known."

"And the city." Manhunter said.

"What city?" Fable questioned.

"The city of the Devilhunter."

"D.C.?" Abraham said. "You're serious?"

"I am."

Fortune looked at everyone and took in the knowledge from Outlander and Manhunter.

"Then it's settled. We split into two teams. One takes the wilderness. The other enters Washington D.C."

"I'll return to D.C." Abraham said. "Who's coming with?"

"I'm in." Vail said.

"So am I." Cinderella said.

"I will join the three of you into D.C." Manhunter said.

Fortune nodded.

"Well, that leaves myself, Creed, Chaser, Shaw, and Outlander. I guess we'll head into the wilderness. See what we find."

"Let's get started." Vail said, walking towards the doors.

IV

THE WILDERNESS AND THE CITY

Fortune's team, consisting of Creed, Chaser, Shaw, and Outlander entered the wilderness of Washington D.C. in the late hours. Fortune moved through the forest, using his magic to scan the areas in their presence. The others were doing the same in their own way.

"What are we looking for?" Chaser asked.

"Something that will lead us to the source of the darkness." Fortune answered.

"Does it have an appearance of its own?" Shaw questioned. "Is it an object or something within the air?"

"I'm not certain."

They continued to move though the forest, however something lurked behind them in the far distance. Keeping a keen gaze upon them like a predator towards its prey.

Elsewhere, Vail's team, consisting of Abraham, Cinderella, Fable, and Manhunter began a search throughout D.C. No other civilians were roaming the streets. It was surprisingly silent and clear. Going from street to street in the hopes of uncovering some strange disturbances. Yet, they found none.

"Which other districts should we check?" Cinderella asked.

"You think we should check out that White House you guys are famous for?" Fable said.

Vail and Abraham turned toward Fable with stares and no expression. Fable nodded, seeing if they would agree. They refused and turned back toward their own direction. Fable shook his head with a shrug of the shoulders.

"What of Foggy Bottom?" Vail asked.

"You think something could be lurking there?" Abraham asked.

"There's a chance. A chance any of the neighborhoods might have something moving around them in the night. We just have to check them out."

"Very well." Manhunter said, conjuring a portal.

The team searched Foggy Bottom and found nothing. They moved through the other neighborhoods with only the same result.

"Are you guys sure this is the city?" Fable asked. "Like could it be a close town or something because we've found nothing."

"We know." Vail said. "Whatever it is lurks in this city."

In the wilderness, Fortune's team moved with ease as the air around them began to thicken. With their senses, they knew something was following them in the night. Shaw turned around after hearing a whisper.

"I can hear you." Shaw said.

"What do you hear?" Fortune asked.

"He hears her." Outlander said, pointing in the direction.

"Her?" Fortune said.

"I can see her as well." Creed said.

"As can I." The Chaser replied.

Fortune stepped forward, gazing in the darkness of the wilderness. Mystical shields formed upon his forearms as his eyes glared with a magical gaze.

"Whomever you are, step out from the darkness."

Moving from the darkness was the woman. Dressed in her red trench coat and black dress. She hovered above the ground with a smirk across her face. She stopped and faced the team. A laugh exhaled from her mouth to their displeasure.

"Who are you?" Fortune asked.

"Wait. You don't know who I am?"

"Should I?"

"She is Elizabeth Bathory." Outlander said. "The one and only."

"Countess." Fortune said. "I find it strange to see you out here in the middle of the night, following us."

"You're trespassing in matters that do not concern you."

"What matters?"

"The darkness. Gascoyne. You do not understand the work he's seeking to accomplish."

"You know Mordecai Gascoyne?" Shaw said.

"I do."

"Then you can tell us where he is."

"I'm afraid I'm not going to do that."

"I think you will." Fortune said as the glow of the shields increased.

Elizabeth only stared and remained silent. Shaw had enough as he went to strike Bathory with a gust of wind. The wind blew through the wilderness and it did not faze her nor made her move. The Chaser followed with a whip of sinfire. The flames did not scorch Bathory nor left burn marks upon her attire. Creed went and sought to attack her with his own cryptic energy. However, the energy had no effect. Surprising them all, Fortune had enough and from his fingers, he fired a blast of energy. The energy warped around Bathory, revealing an invisible force field.

"Such is explained." Outlander said.

"She's conjured a force field." Fortune said. "We need to take it down."

The team continued their attacks one after the other as a means of shattering the force field surrounding Bathory. With the attacks ongoing, she giggled and remained calm. From the sinfire to the gusting wind to Fortune's own attacks, Bathory savored the moment. Outlander did not attack. He only watched. Watched with a keen eye.

"How come you do not attack?" Fortune asked Outlander.

"My attack is coming. He's on his way."

"Who's on their way?"

"An ally in the field."

The attacks continued against Bathory's shield. No cracks were formed from the energies surrounding it. Outlander glared toward the ground as it began to quake. Catching the others off guard, Outlander commanded them to move as the ground opened up. Bathory watched as the dirt arose from the ground and in the midst of the rising soil was the Mutant-Thing. Standing tall over Bathory. Glaring down at her with his red eyes. His body blending in with the soil.

"This your 'ally in the field'?" Fortune asked.

"He will handle this. We have other matters to attend to."

The Mutant-Thing continued its stare-down with Bathory. She did not move. No fear was seen in her eyes and the Mutant-Thing could sense it. Fortune's team took their leave with Outlander leaving last, keeping his eyes focused on Mutant-Thing and Bathory.

"I do not fear you, Earth-Dweller." Bathory spoke.

"You're trespassing. Leave and never return."

"I'll leave when I choose to leave."

With a low growl, the Mutant-Thing stretched his right arm

and slammed it atop Bathory's shield. Realizing the shield was present, his attacks grew and increased in strength. Outlander watched as Mutant-Thing began to shatter Bathory's shield. The shield showed signs of weakness as the Mutant-Thing drove a punch into the shield, cracking it in Bathory's face. Her eyes widen and she backed away, disappearing in a mist of the night. Silence filled the woods with the Mutant-Thing searching for her. Unable to find her, he turned round to see Outlander still standing.

"I thank you for the call."

"It is my duty." Outlander said. "I know we'll run into her again."

"If you're out in the wilderness of the earth, I shall lend my hands to this battle."

"I understand."

The ground opened as the Mutant-Thing stepped down, returning into the soil and the Outlander disappeared with only a subtle flash of light.

Back in D.C., the team moved and discovered nothing. Seeing it all as a dead end, they decided to return to Abraham's Center and upon their decision to return, a snarling screech echoed through the empty streets, pausing the group where they stood.

"You all heard that right?" Fable asked.

"We did." Abraham said. "What was that?"

"Only way to find out." Vail said, walking forward. "Whoever you are, come on out and greet us."

With Vail's permission and from around the corner of a nearby building came two figures. They moved slow, yet their intelligence was noticed. Vail nodded at the sight while Abraham and Fable slowly took steps back. Manhunter moved forward, standing beside Vail and Cinderella didn't know what to make of it.

"What are those?" Cinderella asked.

"I'm not certain." Abraham said.

"I know what they are." Vail said. "They're demons. Our personifications of demons."

Vail recognized them as one of the demons appeared to look like Abraham and the other appeared as Vail. Both in dress and body. Their flesh appeared decayed and burnt as were their clothing. Scorched and torn. The demons stopped in the street, facing the team.

"Tell us your names." Vail said.

"I am Liav Sivart." The Vail demon said.

"Maharba Leirbag." The Abraham demon answered.

Vail chuckled.

"Funny. Your names are ours. Only in reverse. Cleaver for a typical demon to make. Tell us why you're interfering in our affairs?"

"We don't answer to you."

"Oh, I think you do. You're sharing my name around, lad. Best you give us some details we can use on our case."

"The darkness will prevail." Maharba said. "It is fate written."

"Nah." Vail said. "I think not."

The demons snarled. Their eyes glared blood red as their hands trembled as if they were in the cold. Their jaws gnashed. Manhunter stared and had enough.

"Return to your dimensions."

With a wave of his hand, Manhunter sent the demons back to their own estates. Clearing the road of their presence. Vail looked back at Manhunter, nodding with a grin. The others were glad the two doppelganger demons were gone. Fable mostly.

"So, what the plan now?" Fable asked.

"We return to the Center." Abraham said. "Figure this out another way."

"I agree." Vail said.

V

THE SOURCE

Everyone had regrouped back inside the Center. Some sat inside the lobby, others in the nearby offices. Outlander and Manhunter remained outside, standing atop the building, overlooking the city. Vail, Abraham, Cinderella, and Fortune remained inside Abraham's office. Abraham grabbed a book from the shelf, sitting down at his desk as he opened it.

"What's that?" Vail asked.

"It's a grimoire. Apparently deals with everything pertaining to darkness."

"So, what are you going to do?" Fortune wondered.

"I can perhaps find something to trace he source of the darkness directly. If there is something here, it can lead us directly to Gascoyne."

"Let me have a look."

Abraham slid the book toward Fortune. He began to turn the pages, searching for the right option. Turning continuously, Fortune had come to a stop. He read the page and closed the book.

"What did you find?" Vail asked.

"The answer to our problem."

"Did you find a solution?" Abraham asked.

"It will suit our cause."

Fortune turned and exit the office with the others following. Abraham asked Fortune where he was going, yet Fortune said not a word. Vail chuckled as he's familiar with the Supreme Enchanter's work in the field. Fortune stepped out of the Center and levitated to the top, seeing Outlander and Manhunter present. He nodded.

"Pardon me, but I'm going to need the roof for a second."

"We are aware." Outlander said.

"By all means." Manhunter replied. "Lead us to the darkness."

Fortune nodded as the two spiritual advisors took their leave. Fortune raised up his arms. His hands opened as if he's reaching for energy. His eyes gazed up into the starry sky. From there, the others stood outside to watch. Fortune began reciting the page from the book in a language unfamiliar to their ears aside from Outlander and Manhunter. Above the sky cracked with a move of thunder and lightning fell, forming a trail of dark mist. The mist moved through the night sky, glowing like starlight. Fortune's pupils were gone and what remained appeared to be galaxies. Fortune stood still for minutes until the cloud was out of their sight. With another stroke of lightning, Fortune awoke from his place and sighed. Lowering his arms and closing his hands. He looked down at the others and gave them a sign of safety. Levitating back to the ground, Vail approached him.

"What did you see?"

"I saw Gascoyne. I saw Bathory. I saw your Emblem. They're in London."

"Seriously." Cinderella sighed.

"Then we know where we must go." Fable said. "Anyone want to open a portal now or something?"

Fortune turned and the portal was opened. The team was ready.

VI

MAGICKS AND MYSTICISM

Through a portal conjured by Fortune, the team arrived in London. Finding themselves standing atop a building overlooking the city. Cinderella moved forward, scouting the area. Shaw moved toward the other corner of the roof.

"What are we to look for?" Vail asked.

"Follow the trail in the sky." Fortune answered, pointing up.

Vail glared up, seeing the same trail from D.C. The trail moved through downtown London, not making a stop.

"We need to follow the trail." Fortune said. "Let's keep moving."

The team followed the trail using portals to travel through London. Inching near the edge of the city, the team came to the outskirts where the darkness fell upon the entrance into a cave. Vail nodded as the mist evaporated into the ground directly at the cave's entrance.

"Think we've found the place?" Vail asked.

"There's no other choice." Fortune answered.

Shaw stepped forward. His eyes locked on the cave's entrance. His eyes flickered through the gaze. Hearing whispers moving past him like a small brush of the wind.

"He's inside."

"Who's inside?" Fable asked.

"Gascoyne and the others."

"Ah." Abraham said. "All in one place."

"Makes this all the better." Vail chuckled.

Walking inside the cave, they found three other paths.

"Everyone knows what we have to do." Fortune said.

"Myself, Cindy, and Gabe will take the left path." Vail said with a point.

"Fable, you're with me, Shaw, and Creed." The Chaser noted.

"Sure. Sure."

"That leaves the two of you with me." Fortune said to Outlander and Manhunter.

"Let us begin." Manhunter replied.

They moved through the paths. The first one with Vail, Abraham, and Cinderella came to a stopping point as they found themselves staring at a room covered with blood across the walls. The floor marked with a pentagram. Vail scoffed as he shook his hands, ready for the confrontation. Abraham sighed as he prepared himself.

"This seems like your department." Cinderella said.

"No worries, Cindy." Vail chuckled. "It is."

From the pentagram came forth fire. Stumbling the three backwards near the entrance. Using his arms to guard his eyes from the flame, Vail looked toward the fire and saw a figure emerge. Within seconds, the flames disappeared and the figure remained. The three saw a woman standing where the pentagram once was centered. The symbol was scorched and evaporated. Vail looked toward the figure, which was a woman.

"The hell's your name?"

"You speak to royalty in such a manner?"

"Royalty? How can that be?" Vail asked. "Are you some kind of princess or something?"

"You do not know your master?"

Vail let out a small chuckle, gazing over toward Abraham and Cinderella while gesturing a pointing finger.

"I'm afraid you're not my master, lass."

"No one dares speak to Elizabeth Bathory in such manner!"

"Elizabeth Bathory?" Cinderella said.

"She's the Countess?" Abraham asked.

"Ah." Vail sighed. "Figured as much. Red clothing and all. Hey, why are you here anyway? Friends with Gascoyne or something?"

"Gascoyne understands my purpose and I understand his. Together, we will reshape this world into our own making."

"I think not."

In the second path, Chaser, Creed, Fable, and Shaw stepped forward, finding themselves in a room with a portal into the Rift pulsing against the wall facing the entrance. Fable pointed toward the portal, knowing what it is.

"We need to shut it."

"I'll give it a try." Chaser said as his hands were consumed with sinfire.

The Chaser approached the portal, setting his hands in a fire-motion. Before the flames could touch the portal, Emblem bolted from the Rift, knocking the Chaser back near the team. Emblem stood, staring at the four members with a grin.

"He's here?" Fable said. "Seriously."

"Who's this guy?" Shaw asked.

"I am Emblem. The new ruler of these lands."

"This is the guy Fable told us about." Chaser said. "We have to take him down."

"It'll take all of us." Fable noted.

"Only way we'll know is by making the attempt." Creed said.

"I am prepared."

"I am intrigued you've found new allies, Kurt Wesker of the Human Realm." Emblem said. "However, without Pandora by your side, how can you truly defeat me?"

"Well, you haven't met these guys. So, they'll show you how we'll win this."

In the third path, Fortune, Outlander, and Manhunter walked into the third room. Seeing a long table with a dozen chairs. On the walls were set chains, skeletons, and symbols of the mystic arts. Fortune knew the symbols as did Outlander and Manhunter.

"They're here." Outlander said.

"They?" Fortune asked. "What do you mean?"

From behind them entered Gascoyne. Cloaked in a white hood, equipped in black-clad armor that resembled the rocks from an erupted volcano. Gascoyne stared at the three and scoffed with his voice. A breath of disgust.

"You must be Mordecai Gascoyne." Fortune said. "I am Doctor Donald Fortune, Supreme Enchanter of this world and I've come to end your darkness."

"A Supreme Enchanter? I've never encountered one before."

"You have now."

"You really believed I would be here alone, only to be attacked by three others? Nonsense."

Behind Gascoyne entered Dr. Geoff Hoff. Fortune, Outlander, and Manhunter remembered him as the leader of the Mythologists. Hoff nodded toward Gascoyne as they faced the three.

"If it's a fight you desire, we shall grant you one."

Back in the first area, Vail, Abraham, and Cinderella clashed their own skill set against Bathory. The Countess used her shielding to deflect the fireballs from Vail as Abraham set forth to summon fire from below, unable to burn through the shield. Cinderella had no other means than to attack the shield head-on.

"We need something stronger." Abraham said.

"I know." Vail said. "But, what can we use with such strength?"

In the second area, Chaser, Creed, Fable, and Shaw used their own mystic might against the magical powers of Emblem. The portal into the Rift still sat open as Emblem relished the battle. Seeing powerful enemies gave him a sense of peace. A sense of enjoyment.

"This one is strong." Chaser said.

"It must be the portal." Creed noted. "He's siphoning the energy from within the Rift."

"Shit." Fable said. "You're right."

"Best we take one attack each upon the portal." Shaw said. "Shatter it from the wall."

Creed flew toward Emblem, dodging his energy blasts as he clawed the wall, cracking it in a corner and the portal flickered. Chaser threw several balls of sin fire, burning the wall, melting it and the portal flickered faster with continuous flashing.

In the third room, Fortune clashed with Gascoyne as Outlander and Manhunter easily handed Hoff as he had no abilities.

"Should we aid the Enchanter?" Manhunter asked.

"He will take care of Gascoyne easily." Outlander said. "We know his power."

While they stood, a strange gust of wind moved through the

caverns. Entering all three points of entry. The wind was peculiar in such a manner it even caught the attention of Outlander and Manhunter. They looked toward one another with strange gazes. The wind was beyond even their own power.

"Someone else is here." Outlander said.

The wind grew stronger in the first room as Bathory's shield was still intact. The wind made its move and attacked Bathory, easily shattering the shield as it knocked her against the wall. Vail, Abraham, and Cinderella looked as the wind merged into a shadow of pure darkness, forming itself into a physical entity. Abraham and Cinderella weren't sure what it could be, but Vail knew and he smirked.

"Spirit-Seeker."

"Didn't think I would see you again." Vail said.

The entity turned around. Revealing itself to be none other than Darkous of the Astrals. He looked toward Vail and nodded. Darkous transformed into the mist of darkness, bolting from the room.

"Who was that?" Cinderella asked.

"He's a old friend."

In the second room as the portal to the Rift was nearing its destruction, Emblem's power increased as he knocked down Fable and Shaw. He fought against Creed and the Chaser as the mist of darkness entered, snatching Emblem by his neck and slamming him into the ground, causing a small quake, breaking the portal from the wall. Emblem glared up to see the manifestation of the mist and fear snatched him by his throat.

"What are you?"

"I am what you fear. What those of your nature fear. I am

darkness incarnate."

Fable and Shaw stood up next to Chaser and Creed as Darkous revealed himself to them.

"A pleasure to see you. The Man Called Fable. A Soul of Retribution. And an Unholy Knight."

"Same here, my guy." Fable said with no amusement.

Darkous nodded and left.

In the third room as Gascoyne began to manage to take down Fortune, Darkous entered, startling Gascoyne in his steps.

"You're different than the others." Gascoyne said.

"I am. Because I am beyond those you call master and those who serve you. I am what has been and shall ever be. I am true darkness."

"I will not be going out easily."

"You have no say in such a matter. The darkness has called you."

Darkous rushed with speed, taking Gascoyne by the neck as he began to open a portal of his own. Darkous held Gascoyne in the iar as Mordecai did his best to fight back. His attacks had no effect on the Keeper of the Cosmos and Darkous tossed the sorcerer into the dark pit. Him and Hoff. Darkous closed the portal as Fortune arose from the ground.

"An Astral." Outlander said.

"I did not expect this." Manhunter said.

Fortune gathered himself as he stared at Darkous.

"An Astral? Here on the earthly plane."

"I am Darkous of the Astrals and I've come to end this false darkness created by sorcerers and evildoers."

"Thank you for your help."

"Who sent you here?" Outlander asked.

"The Master" Darkous answered. "Now, I must take my leave.

We will all meet again. One day."

Darkous vanished through the mist as the team regrouped. All telling their tale of witnessing Darkous' power. From there, Emblem was sent to the Hidden Four with the aid of Fortune. Bathory was sent to a magical prison and Gascoyne and Hoff remained missing from the earth.

After the team each returned to their own estates of operations, Fortune worked within the Citadel, reading about the Astral entities as he sought to learn more about them. More so about Darkous than the others. While reading, a knock came from the front doors. Fortune arose and answered the door, finding a man atop a white horse. Attire similar to the early Medieval period. Long red robe and folded hat. He carried a golden staff.

"Who are you?" Fortune asked.

"I am the Pardoner and I've come with offering in which you may have interest."

THE DARK TITAN UNIVERSE CONTINUES IN:

BOOK 10

ABOUT THE AUTHOR

Ty'Ron W. C. Robinson II is the author of several works of fiction. Including the *Dark Titan Universe Saga, The Haunted City Saga, EverWar Universe, Symbolum Venatores, Frightened!, Instincts,* and others. More information pertaining to the author and stories can be found at darktitanentertainment.com.

Twitter: @DarkTitan_
Instagram: @darktitanentertainment
Facebook: @DarkTitanEnt
Pinterest: @darktitanentertainment
YouTube: Dark Titan Entertainment

www.ingramcontent.com/pod-product-compliance
Lightning Source LLC
LaVergne TN
LVHW041845070526
838199LV00045BA/1438